THE
FLOODS
4

Survivor

THE FLOODS

4
Survivor

Colin Thompson

illustrations by the author

RANDOM HOUSE AUSTRALIA

This work is fictitious. Any resemblance to anyone living or dead is purely coincidental.

Random House Australia Pty Ltd
Level 3, 100 Pacific Highway, North Sydney, NSW 2060
http://www.randomhouse.com.au

Sydney   New York   Toronto
London   Auckland   Johannesburg

First published by Random House Australia 2007

National Library of Australia
Cataloguing-in-Publication Entry

 Thompson, Colin (Colin Edward).
    Survivor.

    For primary school children.
    ISBN 978 1 74166 129 3 (pbk.).

    1. Witches – Juvenile fiction. 2. Wizards – Juvenile fiction.   I. Title.
    (Series: Thompson, Colin (Colin Edward) Floods; 4).

    A823.3

Design, illustrations and typesetting by Colin Thompson
Additional typesetting by Bookhouse, Sydney
Printed and bound by Griffin Press

15 14 13 12

The Floods' Family Tree

MERLIN
Wizard

MORDONNA
Witch

Valla
Boy - 22

Satanella
Girl - 16

Merlinmary
Not sure - 15

Winchflat
Boy - 14

Morbid & Silent
Twin boys - 11

Betty
Girl - 10

Spot The Difference

Here are the Hulberts before they met the Floods.

Here are the Hulberts after they met the Floods.

Can you spot the 2,873 differences between the two pictures?

Turn to page 204 to find the answers.

Prologue

If you haven't read the first three Floods books, you are probably feeling like you are a complete failure, which of course you are. However, it's your lucky day because there is a way to stop being a failure and start living a full and fantastic life. All you have to do is read the first three Floods books.

If you borrow them from a library or a friend, that's fine – though if you go out and buy them, then you will become a totally brilliant person and are guaranteed to be a huge success, incredibly popular, stunningly rich and good looking.

Yes, it's true, all these great achievements can be yours simply by buying your own copies of the three Floods books that came before this one.

However, if you are too poor or mean or lazy or Belgian or simply impatient to bother with the first three books, this is what you have missed . . .

The Floods are a family of witches and wizards who live in Acacia Avenue – an ordinary street in an ordinary town, just the sort of place you and I might live. The first Floods book is called **Neighbours** because it's all about the neighbours from hell who live next door to the Floods. You will be delighted to know that by the end of the book, the nasty neighbours have all been disposed of in suitably nasty ways.

Nerlin and Mordonna Flood have seven children. The eldest, Valla, has left school and is the manager of the local blood bank, a job he got by draining the blood out of the previous manager and all the other applicants who applied to replace him.[1]

---

[1] *Don't try this at home.*

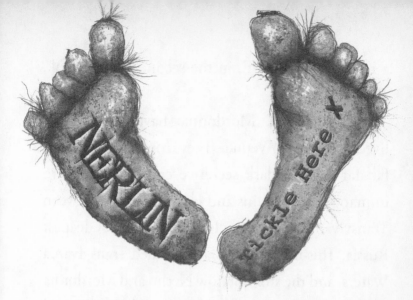

The little number you can see at the end of the previous sentence refers to a footnote at the bottom of this page. It does not mean there is something written on your foot, though Nerlin actually does have his own name written on the bottom of his foot in case he forgets it, or worse still loses his foot. Of course, if he loses the foot that doesn't have his name written on it, then he'll have to hop everywhere.

The next five children go to a wonderful school for witches and wizards in Patagonia. Their school is called Quicklime College. You can read about this school, which makes Hogwarts look like

a really boring TAFE, in the second Floods book, *Playschool*.

Nerlin and Mordonna have not always lived in Acacia Avenue. They come from a land far, far away, a dark secretive country hidden in unmapped mountains and gloomy valleys between Transylvania and the endless pine forests of deepest Russia. This mysterious place is called Transylvania Waters, and the story of how Nerlin and Mordonna met, fell in love, escaped, fled round the world, had several children and ended up in Acacia Avenue is all written down in the third Floods book, ***Home & Away***.

Betty, the youngest of the Floods, goes to an ordinary school just down the road, like you might go to. You can read about it by turning to the next page and moving your eyes backwards and forwards until you have read all the words. Then turn the page over and keep on reading until you reach the end of this book.

Right, off you go . . .

When Betty Flood was born, there wasn't a single child the same age as her anywhere in Acacia Avenue. There were some older girls who went past her house each day on their way to school, and there was a strange boy at number 27 who should have gone to school but didn't because his even stranger parents decided they could teach him everything he would ever want to know themselves. Which they couldn't, though the strange boy, Nautilus, did know much more about earthworms than anyone else in the town, apart from his father, who obviously knew a bit more because he had taught

Nautilus. Nautilus also knew an amazing amount of stuff about slugs, which his mother had taught him, but he didn't know how to cover them in chocolate and turn them into delicious snacks like Betty and her mother, Mordonna, did.

Nor did Betty have any cousins to play with. In fact, she didn't even know if she had any cousins. Her mother said Betty had an Aunt Howler back in Transylvania Waters, but Mordonna thought it very unlikely that Howler had married. If she did have children they probably wouldn't be the sort of cousins Betty would want to play with, unless she was wearing a radioactive protection suit and enjoyed being bitten by things with green teeth. Betty's father, Nerlin, wasn't sure if he had any brothers or sisters because his parents didn't like to talk about that sort of thing.

As soon as she was old enough to do stuff in the kitchen, Betty decided to make her own friends. She made gingerbread friends with currants for eyes, in a tin that had enough room to make six friends at a time. After Betty had eaten five of them, she

took the last one up to her room and, because she was a witch and could do magic stuff, she made it come to life.

At first it was great having a little friend to talk to and play with. Betty dressed it up in dolls' clothes and the two of them ran around the garden chasing butterflies and birds, though sometimes the birds turned and chased Betty's little playmate and tried to peck out its currant eyes – especially the magpies, which are famous for liking currants and sultanas.

The trouble was that although she had made the gingerbread friend come to life, it still smelled like gingerbread. So as the afternoon wore on and lunchtime became further and further in the past and teatime was still a long way off, Betty began to get hungry. She kept looking at her little friend happily skipping through the grass, leaving a trail of crumbs behind it, and instead of dressing it in tiny frocks and tucking it up in bed, Betty wanted to bite its head off and tuck it up in her tummy. Because she was a kind child, Betty turned her friend back into a biscuit before she ate it, but she still felt a bit miserable afterwards.

'Well, it's your own fault,' said Mordonna. 'That's what happens if you eat between meals.'

This went on until Betty was ten years old. One week she made gingerbread girls. Another week she created marzipan twins and then a butterscotch boy, but her favourite friend was meringue man, who was big and bouncy and full of sugar. She tried bringing jelly babies to life, but they were too small to play with and she kept standing on them.

During the summer holidays when Betty had her eleventh birthday, a new family arrived in Acacia Avenue three doors away at number 19.

Mordonna and Betty hid behind a big bush in their front garden and watched as the new family's furniture was unloaded.

There was a man, a woman and two children and they all looked seriously old-fashioned, which is another way of saying **boring**. There was a baby, who was probably a boy, though it could have been either, and there was a girl who looked about the same age as Betty.

'Look, darling,' said Mordonna. 'Someone

your own age to play with at last.'

'Oh yes, wonderful,' said Betty. 'Mr and Mrs Nerd and their nerdy daughter.'

'Now, now,' said Mordonna. 'How many times have I told you that you shouldn't judge a book by its cover?'

'Never, actually,' said Betty, who was not in a good mood. She'd been hoping someone her own age would move into Acacia Avenue, but now it had actually happened the newcomer looked about

as exciting as a wet fish in a bucket of mud.[2]

'I'm sure I have,' said Mordonna. 'After all, look at our family. Just imagine what people would think if they looked at us but didn't really know what we were like.'

'They'd probably think we were a bunch of witches and wizards,' said Betty.

'Well, yes, but . . .'

'Which we are.'

'Yes, I know. But people might look at us and think we do all sorts of weird and dangerous magic,' said Mordonna.

'We *do* do all sorts of weird and dangerous magic,' said Betty.

'Well, yes,' said Mordonna, 'but what I mean is, people would look at us and think we're really evil.'

'But we –' Betty began.

'No we're not,' Mordonna interrupted. 'We're

---

[2] *And of course you should never compare excitement to a wet fish in a bucket of mud. I have at least three cousins who are nowhere near as exciting as a bucket of mud, even one with no fish in it at all.*

really nice. What I mean is, appearances can be really deceptive, darling. Look at your brother Winchflat. Some people would think he was terrifying, but he wouldn't harm a fly.'

'Well, no, he wouldn't harm it, but he might give it an extra head or make it become a metre long,' said Betty.

'By the way, when did you see him last?'

'Can't remember.'

'I think it was nearly a week ago,' said Mordonna, 'when we had those fabulous braised maggots for dinner.'

'I wouldn't worry,' said Betty. 'You know what he's like. He'll be off somewhere creating some brilliant invention.'[3]

'I'm sure he is,' said Mordonna. 'But just remember him when you judge people by their looks. Things are not always what they seem.'

'Yeah, right,' said Betty. 'So you're telling me that we just look like witches and wizards, but really we're all Sunday School teachers in disguise?'

---

[3] *This was exactly what Winchflat was doing.*

13

'Now you're just being silly,' said Mordonna.

'Well, I think the new family look really nerdy and boring,' said Betty. 'So does their furniture.'

'Some people like footstools, darling,' said Mordonna. 'Though I was never a big fan of Skivvytex myself – I find your thighs get all sweaty and stick to it.'[4]

'It reminds me of something,' said Betty.

'Yes, your grandmother's skin.'

'Skin?' What skin? Where?' said Satanella,

---

[4] *Skivvytex is a disgusting leather-look plastic made from environmentally nauseous recycled Belgian beach sandals. Greenies love Skivvytex even though it uses ten times as much energy to recycle it as it would to make brand new plastic.*

who had been burying next door's cat under a camellia bush.

She looked over at the new neighbours. 'Mmm, that baby looks nice. I love babies, they always smell great and have food down their fronts. Yum, yum.'

'Well, I think we should go and welcome them to Acacia Avenue,' said Mordonna.

'No thank you,' said Betty.

'Oh yes you will, young lady, or you'll be in big trouble,' Mordonna snapped.

'Oh, all right, I suppose a nerdy friend is probably better than no friend,' said Betty. 'Anyway, I can always do magic on her.'

'No, you can't. I absolutely forbid it. You know your magic always goes wrong.'

'Not always, but OK,' said Betty. 'I'll bake them a welcome cake, then, shall I?'

'That would be lovely, darling,' said Mordonna. 'Just one thing, though. Until we get to know them a bit better, I'd leave the crystallised cockroaches off the top. Some people are a bit funny about dead insects.'

'So no mouse ears embedded in the icing either?'

'Probably not a good idea. And I'd leave off those little bows you're so good at making out of rat's intestines.'

'OK. I'll just do a plain old chocolate cake,' said Betty. 'Humans seem to like them best.'

Satanella wagged her tail at her mother. 'Can I come with you to meet them, Mum?'

Mordonna patted her on the head. 'No, darling, better wait till we know them a bit better before you start licking their baby.'

Over the next few days, Betty hid up a tree and watched the new girl and her baby brother playing in their back garden. The girl's playing looked very boring, the sort of playing a nerdy girl *would* do. First she skipped round the lawn in one direction five times, then she skipped round in the opposite direction five times. The only time she did anything different was when she tripped on the skipping rope and fell over.

While she did this, her baby brother sat in the

middle of the lawn trying to push grass and worms up his nose. In Betty's eyes this seemed to show he had a more adventurous imagination than his sister. Betty must have climbed up the tree at least ten times that week and every time all she saw was the same, skip, skip, skip, worms up nose, except on Friday. On Friday, the girl tripped and fell on top of the baby, who, at exactly the same moment, had been trying to put yet another worm into his nose. The sudden crashing down of his sister jerked his arm and he swallowed the wriggling worm.

Betty nearly fell out of the tree laughing. Fortunately the baby was crying too loudly for the girl to hear her.

On Saturday afternoon Mordonna put on her least witchy clothes and Betty tied her hair in red ribbons that were not at all the sort of red colour that blood is, and mother and daughter went to visit the new family.

When she had watched them move in, Mordonna had guessed that the whole family was very shy, so she blew a little relaxing-with-witches powder into the air as she rang the doorbell.

'Welcome to Acacia Avenue,' she said, holding out the plate with the chocolate cake.

'Oh, how nice,' said the woman. 'Do come in.'

As the relaxing-with-witches powder went up her nose, she broke out in a big smile. Even the baby, who spent half the day crawling round the floor whinging about biscuits, gazed up at Mordonna and Betty with big happy eyes and only wet himself a little bit.

The new family were called the Hulberts. The baby was a boy. He was fifteen months old and called Claude. The girl was the same age as Betty and was called Ffiona.

Mrs Hulbert explained that Ffiona was called Ffiona and not Fiona because Mr Hulbert wrote with a stutter and that's what he put down when he went to register her birth. Claude nearly got called Cccclaude, but the registrar realised Mr Hulbert had made a mistake and changed it.[5]

If I was called Bbetty, thought Betty, *I'd be really embarrassed.*

But the funny thing was that the name suited Ffiona. She looked just like you would imagine someone with that name would look. Ffiona always had neat polished shoes, tidy school clothes with no bling, no nail varnish and no jewellery. She didn't even have her own mobile or say 'whatever'. She looked like photos of your granny when she was a little girl, and she wore big glasses like your granny wore when she was too old to care about how uncool they looked. The one thing Ffiona did have lots and lots of was freckles. She had hundreds

---

[5] *You may find this hard to believe but there are girls who really do get called things like Ffion and Aaaqil and Ffarjon, especially in Wales, where everyone thinks with a stutter.*

of them. Even her freckles had freckles, and she probably had a jar in the bathroom full of spare freckles for when she got bigger and had more space for them.

'Why don't you take Betty up to your room and show her your toys?' Mrs Hulbert said to Ffiona.

'Umm, all right, Mother,' said Ffiona nervously.

Ffiona was scared of other children her own age, because she had almost never met any who had been nice to her, apart from a few who looked even nerdier than she did and only ever wanted to talk about computer programming and the major exports of Belgium.

So while the two mothers drank their tea and Claude sat on the floor staring at Mordonna and sucking the hem of her dress, which actually contained a chemical that was very soothing for teething infants, Ffiona and Betty went upstairs.

To Betty's surprise, they became instant best friends. This wasn't actually at all surprising because Mordonna had designed a special spell to do exactly that, though of course neither girl ever found that out.

Ffiona told Betty all the sad little secrets she had never been able to tell anyone before.

As everyone knows, kids can be horrible to each other and much more narrow-minded than their parents ever are. They can't stand anyone to be different. So because of her freckles and the lace-up shoes and the tidy hair ribbons, Ffiona's life at school was always made absolute hell by all the other kids. It had been particularly bad at her last school, Thistlecrown Primary. Ffiona's life had been a neverending misery. At least once a week her teacher had to fish her out of the drains after

the bullies had flushed her down the toilet, and it always took the entire summer holidays for her hair to grow back after it had been pulled out or had rude words cut in it on the back of her head.

'And we moved once before that too,' Ffiona explained. 'We came here because Mum and Dad thought it looked like a nice peaceful area and so the school would probably be nice and peaceful too.'

'What, Sunnyview?' said Betty.

'Yes. What's it like?' Ffiona asked. 'Is it nice?'

'Well,' Betty explained, 'all that stuff you said about your old school is pretty much what Sunnyview is like.'

'Oh,' said Ffiona. Her shoulders fell and she began to look miserable.

'But,' said Betty, 'you don't have to worry. I'll look after you.'

'But what about the big kids? Won't they just push us both down the toilet?'

'If you're my friend, no one will lay a finger on you.'

'Why not?'

'Well, it's like this . . .' Betty began.

Having just got her first best friend, Betty was a bit anxious about telling Ffiona she was a witch. But then, she thought Ffiona would find out soon enough anyway, so she went ahead and told her everything.

'A witch? Wow,' said Ffiona. 'Are you sure? My mum says there's no such thing as witches and wizards. She says it's all made up.'

'Lots of it is,' said Betty. 'All that Harry Potter stuff's not real, but there are proper witches and wizards and I'm one.'

'You don't look any different,' said Ffiona. 'I mean, umm, your mother, she kind of does look like, umm . . .'

'She really looks like a witch, doesn't she? All the black hair and eye make-up and deathly white skin?' said Betty. 'Mind you, she could be mistaken for a Goth looking like that.'

'Goths don't wear pointy hats, though, do they?' said Ffiona.

'That's true.'

'But you don't look like your mum,' said Ffiona. 'You look ordinary.'

'I know,' said Betty. 'It used to upset me, but it's actually brilliant, because I can do all sorts of magic stuff and no one ever suspects me because I look like a sweet little girl.'

'Can you really do magic?'

'Yes, it's great,' said Betty.

She told Ffiona that all the kids at school knew she was a witch and left her alone.

'A few of the really stupid kids tried to pick on me,' she explained, 'but after I turned this disgusting boy who used to live next door to us into a fridge, they pretty well leave me alone.[6] So if I let everyone know you're my friend, you'll be OK.'

Ffiona looked so relieved that Betty thought she was going to burst into tears.

'Can you do some magic now?' Ffiona said.

'OK, though you mustn't tell my mum, because she made me promise not to,' said Betty.

She clicked her fingers and Ffiona's Barbie doll leapt off the bed, ran three times round the room and vanished under the bed. Ffiona sat wide-eyed with a huge grin on her face. The Barbie doll crawled out from under the bed, shook herself and jumped up into Ffiona's arms.

'I love you,' said the doll and then turned back into a normal doll.

---

[6] *See* The Floods 1: Neighbours.

'WOW,' said Ffiona, holding the doll up to her face and shaking it a bit.

'Don't do that, you'll give me a headache,' said the Barbie.

'So you needn't worry about anyone bothering you at school,' said Betty. 'And anyway, our school toilets are too small to flush children down.'

'Oh, thank goodness!' said Ffiona. 'Shall we go and ask our mums if you can come and visit again tomorrow?'

'Good idea. But you shouldn't tell your mum about me being a witch,' Betty added. 'Not yet, anyway.'

The girls went back downstairs, where Mrs Hulbert was trying to get Mordonna to be enthusiastic about the joys of crochet. Mordonna was biting her tongue to stop herself clicking her fingers and doing some serious magic. What she wanted to do was make seven sheep appear in the Hulberts' back garden, each one covered in a different very brightly coloured wool. She wanted them to stand in a mystical circle while all their

wool leapt off their backs, spun itself into knitting wool, shot up into the clouds at the speed of light before reappearing thirty seconds later as a massive crocheted blanket that covered the whole lawn.

Instead she drank her tea and ate a coconut biscuit, though she did do one tiny magic trick that made Mrs Hulbert decide to stop buying *Women's Weekly* and buy *Cosmopolitan* instead.

'See, I told you not to judge people by their looks,' she said to Betty as they walked home.

'Yes, Mother,' Betty admitted reluctantly. 'I really like Ffiona.'

'There you go,' said Mordonna, 'and I expect I'll really like Mrs Hulbert too. I must remember to find out what her first name is.'

3

For the rest of the holidays Ffiona and Betty saw each other every day. Betty was rather nervous the first time Ffiona came to her house. After all, not many people have a sister who is a small hairy dog called Satanella.[7] Nor do they have a sister called Merlinmary who is so hairy she might actually be a he, but no one can get near enough to find out in case they get a severe electric shock. In fact, most people don't have any relations as weird the Floods.[8]

---

[7] *Actually, not many people have a sister called Satanella.*

[8] *Though I did have an Uncle Claude who spent the last fifteen years of his life living in a large bucket of preserved eggs*

'Listen, everyone,' Betty said at breakfast the first day Ffiona was coming to visit, 'my new best friend's coming over today and I don't want you all to freak her out.'

'What do you mean?' said Morbid. His twin, Silent, sniggered quietly.

'Come on, you know,' said Betty. 'We don't look like other people and . . . hey, stop doing that.'

Morbid and Silent were making slime appear in midair and then run down all over their faces, and it wasn't nice green slime, it was purple with bits of carrot in it.

'All right, little sister, just for you,' said Winchflat, and he made his left ear – which he had transplanted to the end of his nose to see if it improved his hearing – go back round to the side of his head.

'And I promise I won't do anything like this,'

---

in the mistaken belief that the liquid would also preserve him, which it did. It didn't stop him from dying but it did stop bits of him rotting away after he had died.

said Merlinmary, setting the curtains on fire with a bolt of lightning.

'OK, OK, that's enough, children,' said Mordonna. 'This little girl is quite shy and she is Betty's best friend so let's all be nice to her and act as human as possible.'

'Yeuww, gross,' said Morbid.

Only Satanella didn't do anything silly. She just nudged at Betty's hand and said, 'Is the little baby coming too?'

'No, not today,' said Betty.

Betty had suggested to Ffiona that she might like to leave her glasses off until she got used to the Flood family, but she needn't have worried. Her brothers and sisters had only been teasing and did their best to make Ffiona welcome.

The twins, Morbid and Silent, went as far as falling deeply in love with Ffiona the instant they saw her. It was touching to see their green skin flush pink with shyness. Actually, it wasn't so much touching as weirdly nauseating. Because although pink and green go together quite well in clothes,

they don't look so great on skin. Their adoring gazes looked like a cross between an unwanted puppy, true love and something that had been dead for four days. Fortunately Ffiona did not realise their weird expressions meant they loved her. She just thought they always looked like that.

Ffiona shook all four of the twins' hands about fifty times, and after Betty finally managed to drag her away to meet the rest of the family, the twins

put on rubber gloves and said they would never wash their hands again.

Satanella didn't want to freak Ffiona out by seeming to be a talking dog, so she had managed to type her a card, which she laid in Ffiona's lap. It said:

> Dear Ffonia
>
> Awl though I mite look like er dog, I am achlly a girl so when I tork don't be ~~frihentnd~~ ~~fry tend~~ suprised. My name is Stanella and if you feel like frowing er stick or red borl that wood be grate.
>
> Yore fren
> Staneller
>
> P.S. Don't spose U bort your bruther did U?

'You didn't, did you?' said Satanella.

'Didn't what?' said Ffiona, holding the note at arm's length to avoid its old-bone-been-buried-for-a-while-and-then-dug-up-again smell.

'Bring your baby brother with you?'

'No, he's asleep. He keeps putting worms up his nose and it makes him very tired.'

Ffiona said hello to Winchflat and Valla, and told Nerlin she was pleased to meet him, and she was about to shake hands with Merlinmary but the whole family shouted 'No!' and Betty knocked her to the ground before Merlinmary's friendly lightning could fry Ffiona's eyebrows.

She even shook the skeletal hand of the children's grandmother, Queen Scratchrot, who was buried in the back garden – and she still wasn't put off when she found bits of grey skin under her fingernails. A bit of decomposing flesh on your hands was a small price to pay for having a best friend.

Ffiona also found that the twins bringing her glasses of water garnished with frogs' eyes every five

minutes was better than sitting at home trying to avoid crocheting yet another baby blanket.

'Well, they're actually quite nice,' she said to Betty, who had chased the twins out of the room. 'In a slimy sort of way.'

'Are you sure?' said Betty, who was still worrying her strange family would frighten Ffiona. 'You mean, you actually like them?' She pointed to the frogs' eyes floating in the glass.

'Yes, now I'm used to them,' said Ffiona.

The twins, listening outside the room, thought that Ffiona was talking about them and their hearts

almost burst with love. Their eyes rolled back inside their heads and looked at their brains while brown smoke dribbled out of their nostrils, and as everyone knows, happiness just doesn't get any better than that.

'You know what?' said Betty. 'I think you must have a witch or a wizard somewhere in your family.'

'Do you think so?'

'Well, if you like eating frogs' eyes,' said Betty.

'But I can't do magic or anything like that,' said Ffiona.

'Maybe you've just never been shown how.'

'Could you show me?'

'Oh yes, no problem,' said Betty.

Although Betty said this with great confidence, she had never done anything like it before and she often got magic spells wrong. Once she had tried to turn a pumpkin and four white mice into a carriage and horses like in *Cinderella*, but she had ended up with four geography teachers and a camping

toilet. The toilet was a big hole in the ground and the geography teachers were in the hole up to their necks, which, of course, many people would agree is the best place for geography teachers.

Since then she had been under strict instructions from her family to stick to small magic, like giving people spots and making toast appear in funny and embarrassing places. She was expert enough to always have total control over what was on the toast and would change it depending on the situation.

Naturally she didn't tell Ffiona any of this.

Besides, she said to herself, *teaching someone else to do magic isn't the same as trying to do it yourself.*

Betty's genius brother, Winchflat, had a massive library of magic books in a cellar under the house. There was everything you could ever want to know about magic, from how to turn four geography teachers in a deep smelly hole into a table lamp with choice of lampshade trim, to how to create an entire planet out of 7,653 simple everyday household items.

Winchflat's favourite place was Quicklime College, the school he went to in Patagonia. He loved school so much that during the holidays when he was working in his secret workshop – where he was spending a lot of time right now working on something BIG – he would make it look exactly like his school classroom.

So, while Winchflat was in his secret workshop, Betty and Ffiona went down to his library to find a book on how to teach magic to someone who may or may not have a bit of wizard blood in their veins.

'Nice cobweb,' said Ffiona, stroking a very hairy spider that was sitting on the door handle.

'Thank you,' said the spider. 'Could you move your thumb? It's squashing my third foot.'

'Sorry,' said Ffiona.

'Listen, Serge,' said Betty to the spider. 'You won't tell Winchflat or anyone we've been in here, will you?'

'Well, umm,' said Serge, 'that depends.'

'On what?' said Betty.

'My sore foot,' said Serge.

'What about it?' said Ffiona. 'I said I'm sorry.'

'I know,' said Serge. 'But you have to kiss it better.'

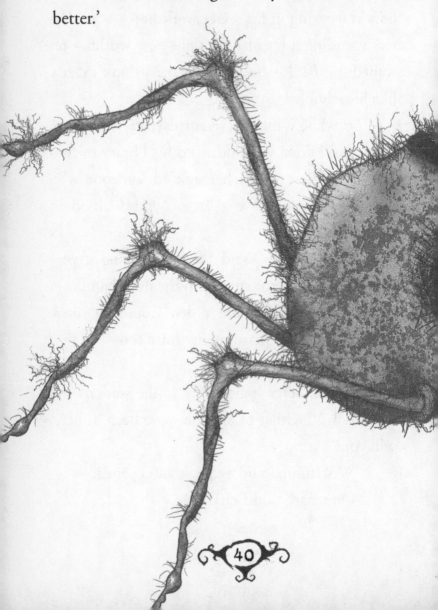

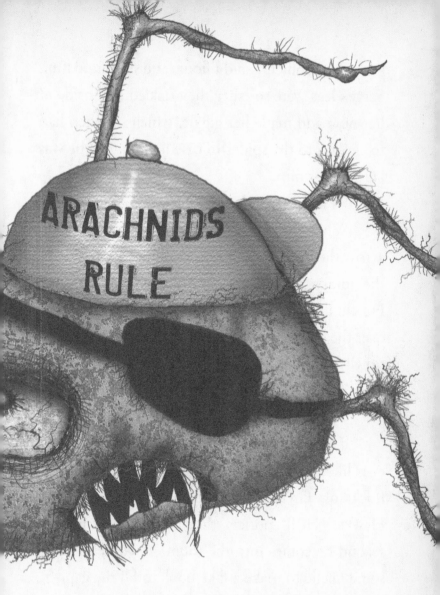

Serge is one of only six known living examples of the rare Patagonian Hairy Toothed Spider. He was smuggled into Acacia Avenue by Winchflat in his school bag.

'No problem,' said Ffiona, and she kissed him. Serge's legs were so hairy they tickled the inside of her nose and made her giggle, which she then had to explain to the spider in case he thought she was laughing at him.

'What are you looking for?' said Serge.

When Betty told him, he ran down the door, across the floor and up to a shelf on the far side of the library to an eighty-five volume encyclopaedia. He climbed on top of the books and disappeared over the back. A few seconds later one of the books slowly moved outwards and fell on the floor.

'Something like this?' he said.

'Brilliant,' said Betty.

'Hold on,' said Serge. 'Your brother has eyes like a hawk. In fact he has eyes like a whole flock of Greater Spotted Tiny Mouse-Eating Hawks. He'll notice the book's missing the second he comes into the room. You'll need to do some magic to make a fake book to fill the gap.'

'Oh right, yes. Err . . .' said Betty, not wanting Ffiona to see how bad she was at magic. 'I'm not

sure I can remember that particular spell.'

'Oh, but surely . . .' Serge began.

'No, I remember now,' said Betty. 'At the end of last term my after-school magic teacher said pretend book spells were the first thing we would do next term.'

'Well, you must be able to do something,' said Serge, but when he saw the expression on Betty's face he realised she hadn't the faintest idea what she was doing.

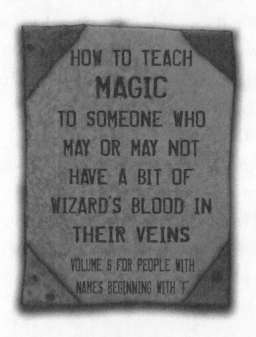

HOW TO TEACH
MAGIC
TO SOMEONE WHO
MAY OR MAY NOT
HAVE A BIT OF
WIZARD'S BLOOD IN
THEIR VEINS
VOLUME 6 FOR PEOPLE WITH
NAMES BEGINNING WITH 'F'

Betty stared at the encyclopaedia and concentrated. Nothing happened. She closed her eyes, except for the corner of the left one, and concentrated harder. Water began dripping out of the ceiling.

'Oops,' she said, but it was too late.

The water ran faster until every one of the remaining eighty-four volumes of the encyclopaedia were soaking wet.

I am in big trouble, Betty thought, *again*.

But the water had done the trick. Each book had swollen up until the gap, where volume six for people whose names begin with 'F' had been, closed up.

'That'll do,' she said.

She clicked her fingers and to her amazement the water actually stopped.

'Well, it will probably fool your brother for a while, at least,' said Serge and, as the two girls left, he climbed onto Betty's shoulder and whispered, 'Your secret's safe with me.'

Back in Betty's bedroom, the two girls sat facing each other on the floor.

'Before we begin,' Betty said, 'I, umm, err, need to tell you something.'

'OK,' said Ffiona.

'I'm not the best witch in the world,' said Betty. 'I mean, sometimes I make tiny little mistakes.'

'Right.'

'What I mean is,' Betty continued, 'my mum has banned me from doing big magic.'

'How do you mean?' Ffiona asked.

'Well, I'm not allowed to change little things like a sparrow into big things like a vulture, because sometimes I get the words a bit muddled up and when you do magic it's really, really important to get all the words right. I mean, you don't just have to use the exact right words, but you've also go to get them in the exact right order, and some of the words are very long and some spells have dozens and dozens of words in them,' Betty explained. 'But of course you can always undo a spell by saying it all backwards.'

'So even if you use all the right words but say them in the wrong order, it can be dangerous?' said Ffiona.

'Not just dangerous, but weird and sometimes even really funny,' said Betty. 'Look.'

She took off her shoes and put them on the carpet in front of her.

'Now what I should say is:

Boring shoes,
Be black no more
With pearls and rubies shine
Boring shoes
Down on the floor
Make yourselves divine.

And then they would turn into a fabulous pair of shiny golden slippers all covered in precious jewels.'

'Wow,' said Ffiona. 'Do it to my shoes.'

'No, because I always get the words muddled up when I'm saying it as a spell. I'll show you

what happens. Oh, and if I were you I'd get up on the bed.'

Betty climbed on the bed too, crossed her fingers and her eyes, which is what you have to do to make ordinary words into a spell, and said:

> *'Boring shoes,*
> *Be black no more*
> *With rearls and poobies shine*
> *Shoring boos*
> *Down on the floor*
> *Make yourselves divine.'*

There was a soft pop and Betty's shoes vanished. A few seconds later there was a lot of thrashing about and strange noises under the bed and a small crocodile appeared.

'See. Now I've go to try and remember what I said wrong and then say it all backwards again to undo it,' said Betty. 'And if I don't get it exactly right, the crocodile will probably turn into something worse.'

The crocodile was scuttling round the room with two Barbie dolls in its mouth. Its tail knocked a chair over and kept banging against the door, until Mordonna called up from the kitchen.

'Betty, have you been playing with your shoes again?'

'Umm, it was an accident, Mum,' Betty shouted.

Mordonna came into the bedroom, grabbed the crocodile by the tail and said, 'Look, that's the third pair of shoes you've ruined in a the past month. You're aired for a week.'

'What's aired?' said Ffiona after Mordonna had taken the crocodile down into the garden. 'I thought it's what my mum did when she hung the blankets out in the sunshine. Your mother's not going to hang you out on the clothesline, is she?'

'No, that's human aired. Witches' aired is like being grounded,' said Betty, 'except your feet don't touch the ground. Look.'

Ffiona got down on the floor and looked at Betty's feet. They were hovering about two centimetres off the ground.

'It means you can't walk anywhere,' Betty explained, 'because no matter how much you move your legs you just stay in the same place. The only way to move around is to grab hold of things and pull yourself along.'

'Couldn't you fly around on your broomstick?'

'What broomstick?' said Betty.

'Don't all witches and wizards have broomsticks?'

'Not nowadays,' said Betty. 'I think my granny might have had one, but we all use vacuum cleaners now.'

'What, to fly on?'

'No, to clean the carpet.'

'I could pull you along,' said Ffiona. 'You'd just have to hold my hand.'

'Not a good idea,' said Betty. 'My mum's already thought of that one. If you hold my hand you'll get a terrible electric shock.'

'Are you sure?'

'Yes, I grabbed Satanella's tail once and she grabbed Merlinmary's ear and we blew all the lights in the street out,' said Betty.

'Oh my goodness,' said Ffiona.

'Actually it was brilliant, but I got into real trouble,' said Betty. 'Mum made me eat porridge for a week.'

'What's wrong with that?' said Ffiona. 'I like porridge.'

At last Betty understood how it was that Ffiona accepted all her strange relations so easily.

If she liked porridge she was weirder than all of them.

Being aired for a week turned out to be quite a good thing. Ffiona came round early every day and she and Betty sat on the bed and read the encyclopedia. Progress was slow because almost every sentence had at least two words neither of them could understand, even though Ffiona was one of those strange children who read dictionaries for a hobby.

'Some of these words aren't even in my dictionary,' she said. 'I mean, what's a starboardcullis? I know what a portcullis is, but I've never heard of a starboardcullis – and how can you tell if it's ripe or not?'

'I think we'll just have to ignore the bits we don't understand,' said Betty. 'We'll leave them out.'

'But the instructions are very precise,' said Ffiona. 'It says we need thirty-seven point eight grammettes of ripe starboardthingies or else the spell won't work, and it says that if we don't do this spell first then none of the other ones will work either.'

'OK, well, when we find come to an ingredient that we haven't heard of,' said Betty, 'we'll try to guess what it might be and use the nearest thing.'

'Isn't that a bit dangerous?' said Ffiona. 'If my mum's cooking something and she doesn't have the right ingredients and uses something else, it always tastes dreadful. I mean, you could think you're making me into a witch and I could end up as a pink rabbit.'

'No way,' said Betty. 'The pink rabbit spell is completely different. I'm quite good at that one except I'm colour blind and my rabbits come out green. I think.'

'I know what a starboardcullis is,' said a voice from under the bed.

'Morbid?' said Betty.

She took her junior witch's pointy stick and poked it under the bed.

'Oww, get off,' said Morbid.

Silent said nothing, because he never did, but he thought, *Oww, get off.*

The twins crawled out covered in fluff and knelt by the bed gazing up adoringly at Ffiona.

'I don't suppose you've got a sticking plaster, have you?' said Morbid. 'That crocodile under there bit my leg.'[9]

'No I haven't,' Betty snapped. 'What were you doing under my bed? You know the rule, none of us is allowed to go into anyone else's room.'

'We came in to see if there was anything Ffiona needed,' said Morbid.

'Well, there isn't. Go away. Ffiona's *my* friend. You go and find one of your own.'

'But . . . but . . . but . . .' said Silent and everyone's jaws dropped.

It was the first time in his entire life that Silent had uttered a a single word. Until then the only way he had ever communicated was by a few grunts, which only Morbid could understand. No

[9] *Although Mordonna kept taking the crocodile away from Betty, she never took it far enough and, being addicted to the fluff from Betty's socks, which collected under her bed, it always found its way back there.*

amount of magic had ever managed to change this, but now he was so infatuated with Ffiona it had given him the power of speech.

'What did you say?' said Betty and Morbid.

'Umm . . . but, but, but,' said Silent.

When they went downstairs and told Mordonna, she was so delighted that she gave Ffiona a huge hug and told her she was the cleverest girl in the world and that she could come and visit whenever she wanted. She even gave Betty her shoes back and un-aired her.

'Mum,' said Betty, 'do you think one of Ffiona's distant relatives might have been a wizard?'

'Absolutely,' said Mordonna. 'I mean, look at all the magic we tried to get poor Silent to talk, and then along comes Ffiona and just one look was all it took for him to start speaking.'

Of course, every silver lining has a cloud and after that it was almost impossible to shut Silent up. He talked in his sleep and didn't even stop even when Mordonna made him eat wet concrete. They tried the terrifying putting-a-spoonful-of-Belgian-

porridge-in his-mouth routine, but even that failed. Finally, they stuck his head underwater. No one could hear him when they did that, but they could tell by the way the fish threw themselves out of the pond that he was still talking.

Being witches and wizards, the only other solutions the family could think of were complicated things that involved a lot of magic and singed hair. It was Ffiona who finally came up with the answer. Because Silent never left a gap small enough for Morbid to get a single word in, Morbid stopped

speaking, so they did the obvious thing and simply swapped names.[10]

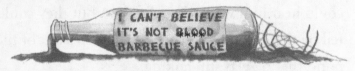

Given Betty's poor success rate with her spells, Betty and Ffiona agreed that they wouldn't try any witch-making magic for the rest of the holidays.

'You should probably get a lot more practice at ordinary magic before we try anything as big as that,' said Ffiona, who was worried that Betty might turn her into a table lamp or a ginger biscuit.

The two girls decided that as they were total and complete best friends, they couldn't have any secrets from each other. This meant that Ffiona had to tell Betty about her 'hankyblanky', which was a disgusting strip of old grey rag she wrapped around her thumb and sucked every night in bed.

---

[10] *Winchflat calculated on his mega-powerful computer that there was a 98% chance of the twins swapping names with each other at last seventeen more times – and that it was quite likely they had done it before.*

She even told Betty that she sometimes picked her nose and ate it.

'Everyone does that, don't they?' said Betty. 'Though I suppose most people don't feed it to their goldfish. Granny Scratchrot collects all the wax out of her ears and the crusty bits from her eyelids and moulds them into little grey mice. Then she picks her nose and makes it into two tiny eyes and when she sticks them on the mouse's head, they come to life and run away down the tunnels that lead to her grave. So I don't think eating the odd bogey matters.'

'What's your biggest secret?' Ffiona asked.

'I don't think I've got one,' said Betty, 'except that I'm not very good at magic, but everyone knows that so it's not really a secret.'

'Haven't you got a hankyblanky?'

'I used to have a dead lizard when I was a baby,' said Betty. 'I used to go to sleep with his tail in my mouth, but when I got my first teeth I ate it in my sleep one night.'

'Is that a secret?' Ffiona asked, thinking that

if she had sucked a dead lizard's tail she probably wouldn't want anyone to know about it.

'Oh no, we all had one when we were babies.'

'I've got another secret,' said Ffiona. 'I'm scared of going to school on Monday.'

'Don't worry,' said Betty. 'I'll look after you.'

Monday morning, 8.25 am – first day of term

Betty kissed her parents goodbye, picked up her school bag and said good morning to the front gate as it opened for her. She turned left down Acacia Avenue on her way to school. As she did so, Ffiona, who had been waiting at her own front gate, came running after her.

'M-m-morning, Betty,' said Ffiona.

Ffiona only stuttered when she was nervous. Her new school uniform didn't help. Most of the other kids had cool shoes, but Ffiona's looked like her granny might have worn them. Most of the

other kids had their hair just hanging down. Some even had it brushed and combed. Ffiona's hair was in two plaits that were so tidy they looked like plastic, with bright red ribbons on each one. And Ffiona's skirt was the only one in the whole school that came down over the top of her really tidy and totally wrinkle-free grey socks.[11]

'Come on,' Betty reassured her. 'I told you there's nothing to worry about.'

As they turned the corner into Juniper Street, four other girls crossed the road and came up behind them. They had learnt long ago to avoid Betty, but since they had never seen her with anyone else, they didn't recognise her at first.

These four girls were Bridie McTort, the school's number one bully, and her cronies. Bridie came from a long line of bullies dating back to the time of her great-grandmother, who liked pulling the wings off butterflies and eating them. As *she* got

---

[11] *One of the teachers, Miss Tankard, always wore a very thick skirt that she could have tucked into her boots, but then her legs were so short there was barely room to fit her knees in.*

bigger, Great-grandmother McTort would pull the wings off bigger things and, by the time she was fifteen, she was chasing swans around the public parks. When she started trying to pull the wings off children, she was arrested and transported to a small remote island, where she pulled the wings off everything – including a small aeroplane, which was pretty stupid as that was the only way of getting off the island. Eventually she was sent back to where she had come from by parcel post. Bridie McTort has a lot of nightmares.

'Oh, look at the little baby with her pretty hair ribbons,' said Bridie, the lumpy one in the middle.[12] 'And look at her little blonde fr–'

She suddenly realised who the little blonde friend was and stopped talking, but it was too late. Betty stopped and turned to face them. The four bullies stepped backwards.

'Stop!' Betty commanded and their legs froze.

---

[12] *I'm sure you've noticed that it's always the shortest one in the middle of a group of bullies who is the biggest coward and does all the talking.*

'Well, well, look who's come to greet us on our way to school,' she continued. 'Beautiful Bridie and her three lovely, lovely friends.'

'We're not scared of you,' said Bridie. 'We know it wasn't you that gave us spots.'

'Really?' said Betty.

'Yeah. It's like, food and stuff that gives you spots, not people,' said Bridie. 'Not even if they're, like, witches, which you're not because there ain't no such thing.'

'Yeah, we're, like, totally not scared of you,' said the other three.

'Well, that just goes to show, and there's no nice way to say this, just how completely stupid you are,' said Betty, 'because you should be. Look.'

And she gave them each fifteen more big painful spots.

'You're a witch, you are,' said Bridie.

'I thought you said there's no such thing?'

'Yeah well, you're, like, totally, I mean, yeah, whatever,' said Bridie.

'Now listen to me, you morons, and make

63

sure you tell all your friends, if you have any. Just
tell them that this is Ffiona and she is my friend
and if she gets the slightest bit of bother from any
of you, I will make you wish you had never been
born,' said Betty. 'Understand?'

The four girls mumbled and looked at
their feet.

'I said, understand?'

More mumbling.

Betty clicked her fingers and five large magpies
landed on a rooftop next to them. Betty pointed up
at the birds and said, 'Do you want my bird friends
to come and pull your hair out?'

'As if,' said Bridie.

'Yeah, like, whatever,' said the other three.

Betty crooked her little finger and beckoned
to the magpies, who all swooped down and began
to attack the four bullies. They were under strict
instructions not to do anything too dreadful like
pecking the girls' eyes out, just to pull their hair
and steal their iPod headphones and burst their
pimples. Betty held up her arms and the magpies

flew over and landed on the fence next to her. She tickled the backs of their heads and gave each one a piece of cheese.

'W-w-wow,' said Ffiona, who had been trying to hide behind Betty and was clenching her hands together really tightly.

The girls ran away across the street and shouted, 'We'll totally get you.'

'Don't you ever learn?' said Betty.

'And we'll, like, get your nerdy friend too, innit?'

Betty walked across to the four girls and stood in front of them.

'Look, I've told you, if the tiniest, weeniest bad thing happens to Ffiona,' Betty warned them, 'you will regret it big time.'

Bridie turned her back on Betty and bent over.

'Like, talk to the bum, because the ears ain't listening,' she said.

'OK, I did warn you,' said Betty. 'And now here's a bum that's much bigger

than yours.'

She held up her left hand and clicked her fingers. An enormous elephant appeared right behind the girls – an enormous elephant that had eaten two hundred kilos of cheap baked beans and hadn't been to the toilet for seven days.

It went to the toilet then vanished.

There was a lot of losing balance and falling over mixed up with a lot of swearing as the four bullies tried to get back on their feet. By the time they managed to crawl away, every single square centimetre of their skin and clothes was covered in elephant poo.

Ffiona couldn't believe her eyes. A big grin spread across her face. It was the sort of grin you get when something incredible happens that you think you might get you into huge trouble, but you still can't stop being excited.

'We know where you live,' the biggest girl cried as the four bullies went home to change. 'We'll get you.'

'In your dreams,' laughed Betty.

Bridie wanted to say, 'I'm telling my mum on you,' but she knew hard girls don't say that sort of thing – and besides, if she had told her mum she would have just got a clip round the ear.

You may well be wondering how Betty managed to do all this stuff to the bullies seeing as how most of her magic always went wrong, and so

it had. All Betty had been planning was for a small black cloud to appear above the bullies' heads and soak them to the skin, with possibly a bit of hail and the odd lightning flash. But Betty was one of those people who often end up better when they make a mistake than when they get things right. The elephant was fifty times better than a bit of rain.

When word got round school about what the elephant had done to the bullies, Betty became a hero. Even the teachers smiled to themselves. Everyone knew that Betty was a witch and that her family were very weird, so they had always kept their distance – especially after the rumours about what she might have done to Dickie Dent. But now everyone wanted to be her friend, if only to make sure the elephant didn't pay *them* a visit. And because Ffiona was Betty's best friend, she was accepted by everyone without all the usual toilet flushing, lunch stealing and hair pulling that usually happened to new girls who looked like Ffiona. Betty was totally cool and that made Ffiona cool too, even if she

did look like she enjoyed embroidery and stamp collecting.[13]

Of course, everyone expected Bridie to try to get revenge on Betty because that's what bullies do, but they also knew that Betty would always win.

'I mean, what can Bridie do?' one of Betty's classmates said to her. 'If she tries to get you into trouble no one will believe her. I mean, who's going to believe an elephant just appeared from nowhere?'

If you look inside most bullies you will find a mean little coward. Some people will tell you it's not their fault that some children are bullies. They might get bullied at home by their older brothers or their parents. Well, like Bridie says: 'Talk to the bum because the ears ain't listening.' Just because

---

[13] *Ffiona's parent thought stamp collecting was a bit too exotic for their family, what with all the bright colours and foreign words on lots of the stamps. They encouraged Ffiona to collect dead leaves, which were nice safe brown colours and had no words or pictures on them at all (apart from one leaf Ffiona's mother had inherited from her grandmother, which actually had a picture on it that looked exactly like the baby Jesus).*

bullies are miserable at home, it doesn't mean they can bully other kids at school.

Bridie *was* bullied at home. She had three brothers who were horrible to her because their dad hit them, and a mother who spent all day at home huddled over a computer trying to steal people's secret passwords and money.[14] But it didn't make it any better for all the kids whose lives Bridie made a misery. If she had had a tiny bit of brain in her head, she would have made friends with Betty and then Betty could have sorted her family out for her.

This is Bridie's brain magnified 3 million times

[14] *So remember, next time you get an email asking you to enter your secret details, it's probably from Bridie's mum.*

But she didn't have any brain. All she had was mean nasty thoughts and all she wanted was revenge. She stayed off school for three days and had to have sixteen baths and a lot of scrubbing before the smell of the elephant finally went. By then her skin and her temper were both red raw and all she wanted to do was kill Betty.

She may have been seriously dumb, but she knew that she would never be able to get the better of Betty. That nerdy new girl, Ffiona, would be a different story, though.

Bridie and her gang made their plans. They went to the hardware store and, while one of the girls fell on the floor pretending to have a fit, Bridie stole six padlocks and some chains.

'No one, like, rags me off and, like, gets away with it,' she said.

'Yeah, like totally whatever, innit?' said her three slaves, though two of them were starting to have second thoughts because, although they would never admit it, they were pretty scared of Betty. Also, after fifteen showers, some of them

with a really hard scrubbing brush, they could still smell elephant poo.

Not only did most of Sunnyview School think Betty was cool, but so did Mrs Hulbert, though cool was not a word she ever used except when she was describing the weather. Mrs Hulbert thought Betty was lovely because when the two girls came home from school that day, Mrs Hulbert thought she had never seen Ffiona so happy. She even got out the chocolate biscuits, which were only for very special occasions like Christmas and birthdays.

'So the new school is wonderful, then, is it?' she said, pretending not to notice when Ffiona gave Betty a second biscuit and took another for herself.

'It is with Betty looking after me,' said Ffiona. She told her mother about the incident on the way to school that morning.

'An elephant, dear?' said Mrs Hulbert. 'Are you sure?'

'Yes, Mother.'

'Gosh.'

Betty was tempted to tell the truth about the elephant being an accident, but Mrs Hulbert said she thought it was quite funny even if it did seem very unlikely, so Betty just drank her glass of milk and kept quiet. She could have explained to Mrs Hulbert that the Floods were witches and wizards, but Betty decided that was something maybe her mother should do. When she got home she told her own mother what had happened before realising she'd been banned from doing any magic, but Mordonna thought it was hilarious.

'We'll make a deal,' she said. 'You *can* do magic, but only when it's to help someone like Ffiona.'

'OK.'

5

Meanwhile, Bridie was making plans for her revenge. Due to her tiny brain, which didn't work very well, the plans were very slow in getting made and were also pretty stupid.

'What we're going to do, like, is, like, kidnap Betty Flood's nerdy friend, yeah?' she said to her three collaborators.

'Right, cool, yeah,' said friend one.

'Totally. I'm, like, yeah, whatever,' said friend two.

'Umm, I've got to go and help my mum,' said friend three, who had a tiny bit more brain than the others.

'No you don't,' said Bridie. 'You're just being chicken.'

'No, no, I mean, yeah, my mum said I've got to go and do a thing for her.'

'If you tell anyone, I will, like, totally kill you,' said Bridie.

'Yeah, yeah, I mean, like, no, I won't tell anyone,' said friend three.

'Well, whatever,' said Bridie. 'Just run away, mummy's bubba, we don't need you anyway.'

'Yeah,' said friend one.

'Yeah, and we, like, never liked you anyway,' said friend two.

When she had gone, the three girls worked out their plan to kidnap Ffiona. The first bit would be the hardest. That was to get Ffiona away from Betty. They walked to school together. They were in the same class all day and then they walked home together.

'OK, like, I've got an idea,' said Bridie.

'Brilliant,' said friend one.

'Yeah, like, yeah,' said friend two. 'What?'

'We have to send a kid to the classroom and say Ffiona's mum needs to see her,' said Bridie.

'What, and we, like, grab her before she reaches her mum?'

'What mum?' said Bridie.

'You said her mum wanted to see her.'

'Not for real, stupid. It's just to get her out of the classroom,' said Bridie.

'But if it's not for real, she won't come,' said friend one.

'She won't know it's not for real. You are, like, so totally dumb sometimes,' said Bridie.

'I don't get it,' said friend two, who was even dumber.

'We need someone to go and do the message,' said Bridie. 'I mean like, none of us can go, 'cos she wouldn't believe us.'

So they got Bridie's little sister – who was also not very bright – and she agreed to go to Ffiona and Betty's classroom the next day to deliver the message, in return for not getting a French burn and ink down her dress.

'I still don't understand how we grab her without her mother seeing us,' said friend one.

Bridie started to explain again, but then gave up. Next to her slaves, she felt really clever. This was one of the two main reasons she had chosen them in the first place. The other reason was that they were the only ones stupid enough to want Bridie as a friend.

'Just leave it to me,' she said, 'and make sure to bring some string and a sack to school tomorrow.'

'My dad's got one,' said friend two. 'I'll borrow his.'

'One what?'

'A sack. I haven't, like, seen it, but I think it's totally brand new because I heard him telling my mum that he got the sack last week.'

'Wow, that is, like, really weird,' said friend

one. 'You don't suppose he knew we would need one and got it specially, do you?'

Bridie closed her eyes and gritted her teeth to stop herself from banging the two idiots' heads together. She started to speak but then thought better of it and just said, 'Yeah, whatever.'

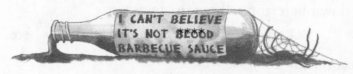

'Come in,' called Mrs Magpie, Ffiona's teacher.

The door opened and Bridie's little sister came in.

'Molly McTort, and what do you want?'

'Got a message, miss,' said the little girl.

'Right.'

Molly nodded and smiled and turned to leave.

'Do you want to give the message to me, Molly?' said Mrs Magpie.

'Umm, umm . . .' said Molly and began to cry.

'It's all right, dear. Nothing to worry about,'

said the teacher, handing Molly a tissue. 'I think you're supposed to give me the message.'

'Get ink on me,' Molly cried and looked like she was about to wet herself.

'No you won't,' said Mrs Magpie. 'No one's going to put ink on you. Now why don't you sit down here and tell me the message.'

'F-f-f-f-f, F-f-f-f, F-f-f, Ffiona mummy here,' said Molly.

'Well done. Well, Ffiona, it sounds as if perhaps your mother's here and wants to see you,' said the teacher. 'Off you go, and drop Molly off at Mrs Dunbarton's classroom on the way.'

Ffiona was very surprised. Not once since her first day at school five years ago had either of her parents ever come to any of Ffiona's schools. They were the sort of people who were a bit scared of teachers and always felt inferior in their presence.[15]

---

[15] *This, of course, is how most teachers want parents to feel and, like doctors, their training includes lessons in how to make people feel silly and inferior. Their argument to support this is that most people really are silly and inferior.*

Even when their poor daughter had been badly bullied, the most they had done was write an apologetic letter to the headmaster – and as everyone knows, any letter written by a parent to their child's school is skilfully and professionally handled by putting it unopened into a rubbish bin where it is dealt with by eventually converting it into compost. Rather than make a fuss, Ffiona's parents just kept moving house.

So it was unheard of for Ffiona's mother to come to school. Even if her granny had dropped down dead, Mrs Hulbert would have waited until Ffiona got home to tell her.

'Are you sure my mother's here?' she asked Molly.

Molly looked as if she was going to burst into tears again, so Mrs Magpie told Ffiona to take her back to Mrs Dunbarton while she rang the front office to see if Ffiona's mother really was there.

As soon as Ffiona and Molly turned the corner towards the kindy classes, Bridie crept up behind them and put the sack over Ffiona's head.

The 'kidnap Ffiona' plan had not included Ffiona screaming at the top of her voice, so when she did, Bridie dropped the rope and the three bullies ran off. By then Molly was crying out loud too and several teachers came out of their classrooms to see what was going on. Having heard the scream, finding Ffiona with a sack in her hand and Molly crying her eyes out, they all came to the same conclusion.

Ffiona had been trying to kidnap Molly.

'Miss Hulbert, you are in big trouble,' said the headmaster when Ffiona was taken to his office. 'In all my years as a teacher, I have never experienced

anything like it. What on earth were you thinking? Were you going to hold Molly ransom?'

'I, no, I . . .' Ffiona began, but no one would let her get a word in edgeways.

'For goodness sake, the McTorts are probably the poorest family in the school,' said the headmaster, adding with a grin to his deputy, 'If I was going to kidnap a child I'd take one of the Huntley-Smiths. They're loaded.'

'No, I, but . . .' Ffiona tried to explain as Bridie and her teacher came into the office.

'She tried to totally kidnap me too, sir,' said Bridie, 'but I managed to escape. I was, like, coming here to get you, sir, when my teacher found me with the spraycan next to the graffiti.'

The headmaster forced himself to try to understand what Bridie was saying, but he was having difficulty.

'Only it wasn't I what done it. It was her,' Bridie went on, pointing at Ffiona. 'I don't never, like, not know what them words she wrote on the wall means.'

The headmaster gave up. They hadn't learnt how to deal with triple negatives in headmaster training.

Then Mrs Magpie and Betty arrived and began to try to straighten things out. The trouble was, the headmaster was one of those pompous sort of people who finds it very difficult to change their minds or ever admit they've made a mistake. As far as he was concerned, Ffiona Hulbert – who was obviously a troublemaker or else she wouldn't have been to so many different schools – had been trying to kidnap sweet little innocent Molly McTort. He managed to overlook the fact that Molly was in training to become a big stupid bully like her older sister and practised each day by picking the scabs off her knees and making other toddlers eat them.

As far as he was concerned, Molly was innocent and Ffiona was a potential gangster terrorist.

'You are suspended pending further investigation,' he said to Ffiona. 'I will need to speak to your parents and maybe even the police.'

The mention of the word 'police' took the

smile off Bridie's face. The McTorts were old acquaintances of the police. At any given time at least three uncles or cousins or nephews were in gaol and the police used to joke that the McTorts had a season ticket to prison. But if Bridie had one talent – and she did only have the one – it was that she was really good at telling lies. Most people usually guessed she was lying about things, but they could never get her to admit it. Some people, like the headmaster, were too lazy to think about it so they just believed whatever she said.

So all of Ffiona and her teacher's arguments fell on deaf ears.[16] He decided to suspend Ffiona because it was the easiest thing to do.[17] When Betty protested, he threatened to suspend her too. Mrs Magpie, who had a soft spot for girls like Ffiona, let Betty out of school early to look after her.

---

[16] *As everyone knows, Deaf Ears are one of the main requirements for someone to become a headmaster. To be a headmistress, you need Deaf Ears and thick lace-up shoes.*

[17] *Training in The Easiest Thing to Do is another qualification required before becoming a school principal.*

'Don't worry,' Betty reassured Ffiona as they walked home. 'It'll all get sorted out.'

'But my parents will be so ashamed they'll have to move again,' said Ffiona. 'And . . .'

'What?'

'I won't see you any more,' Ffiona blurted out, 'and you're the only friend I've ever had.'

'Yes,' said Betty. 'I am your friend and what friends do is look after each other. You must not worry. Your mum and dad won't even know anything's happened at school, never mind want to move. So don't worry.'

One type of magic Betty was always good at was making people feel better and Ffiona put her arm round Betty's shoulder and gave her a big hug.

'You're the best friend anyone could ever have,' she said.

'Yes, I am, aren't I?' said Betty. 'Come on, let's get this sorted out.'

They went into Betty's room and rang the school.

'Headmaster, please,' said Betty, in a voice that sounded exactly how Mrs Hulbert would have sounded if she wasn't as nervous as she was. 'Headmaster? This is Mrs Hulbert. I have just been speaking to my daughter and I am absolutely outraged.'

'So am I, Mrs Hulbert,' said the headmaster.

'Not about the same thing,' said Betty. 'How dare you accuse my daughter of trying to kidnap

one of the worst children in your school? If I don't receive a full written apology and hear that both McTort children have been expelled by tomorrow morning, my brother, the Minister of Education, will hear about it.'

'Oh, er, but, but, but . . .' said the headmaster.

'Impersonating an outboard motor will not help you at all,' Betty continued. 'And quite frankly I am disgusted. I would like you to ponder on what life would be like as the headmaster at the school on St Kilda in the Outer-Outer-Hebrides, a place where the sun seldom shines and all there is to eat are puffins and seaweed.'

'I, umm . . .'

'Never mind that. Do I make myself clear?'

Silence.

'I can't hear you,' said Betty.

'Yes, Mrs Hulbert,' said the headmaster. 'Is your brother really . . .?'

'I do hope you're not suggesting I might be telling lies,' said Betty. 'If that was the case I imagine St Kilda might be too good for you. I'm sure my

brother could arrange a cultural exchange with one of the remand schools in Transylvania Waters.'

'No, no, of course not, Mrs Hulbert,' said the headmaster. 'I'll deal with the McTort girls straight away.'

'My daughter will be back at school tomorrow,' said Betty. 'Think yourself lucky I don't remove her for good. Next time you feel like bullying her, just remember who her uncle is.'

'But I . . .'

'And I'll thank you not to phone me again. You have nothing to say that I want to hear.'

The headmaster began to say that he hadn't phoned in the first place, but Betty had hung up.

'Wow,' said Ffiona, 'that was brilliant, Betty. Do you think it will work?'

'Absolutely,' said Betty.

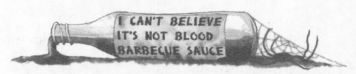

And it had. The headmaster sent for Bridie and told her she had to tell him the truth.

'I never done nothing. It was that witch girl,' said Bridie.

'Which girl?' said the headmaster.

'No, yeah, but no, *witch* girl, stupid, not which girl,' said Bridie.

'Oh, for goodness sake, child, there's no such thing as witches. Just tell me the truth.'

'Yeah, but I, like, come from a broken home,' said Bridie.

'I know that,' said the headmaster, 'but it was you who broke it.'

'So?'

This went on for about half an hour with the headmaster getting nowhere. What he didn't realise was that for Bridie to tell the truth would have been a whole new experience for her and her brain wasn't big enough to fit any new things into. Also, the headmaster kept using words like 'deceitfulness' and 'subversive', which had way too many letters in them for Bridie to have been able to understand them.

The headmaster had never been to Transylvania Waters or even seen a photo,[18] but he

---

[18] *There aren't actually any photos of Transylvania Waters, not because cameras are banned, but because it is so damp there that they go rusty and stop working in less than twenty-four hours. There are a few paintings, but because Transylvania Waters is an enchanted place, if anyone tries to paint something bad, it changes into a pretty landscape with baby rabbits and lovely flowers.*

had heard stories of how an incredibly handsome young student teacher, who may even have been a minor prince, was once sent there and came back six months later as an eighty-five year old Belgian geography teacher with warts.

After an hour of trying to get the truth out of Bridie and failing, he put his head in his hands and said, 'Well, I'm chucking you out of school anyway, and your sister goes too.'

'Cool,' said Bridie defiantly. As she left the room she added, 'Well, yeah, I did do what you said with the kidnap thing and, like, my mum's a gypsy and I'll get her to put a curse on you.'

'Yeah, yeah, whatever,' said the headmaster.

Betty and Ffiona turned up for school the next day and everyone pretended nothing had happened. Not one single teacher said a single word about the incident at the next staff meeting because everyone realised that life was a lot more peaceful without the McTort girls there. Without Bridie's influence the other bully girls kept their heads down and didn't dare bother anyone in case they got thrown

out too. One of them even learned to write her own name in crayon in joined-up writing.

'Yeah, like, the kidnap didn't go totally to plan, but we still, like, got a result,' said Bridie to her two friends when they met at the mall after school, as she used her Tartytat Scarlet Flash lipstick to write something unrepeatable on the window of the 'Happy Babies' nursery shop.

'Oh yeah?' said friend one. 'How was that then?'

'I don't have to go to school no more,' said Bridie. 'That is well cool.'

'Won't your mum and dad, like, go spazz and totally freak out?' said friend two.

'Oh yeah,' said Bridie. 'Like I'm going to tell them, as if.'

'But what about school?'

'Who needs it?' said Bridie. 'Ain't nothing what they can learn me anyway.'

'What, you mean, like, you're not going to tell them and you'll just pretend you're going to school?' said friend two.

'Yeah, whatever,' said Bridie. 'And I'll come down here every day. Brilliant. Anyway, my dad's not there and my mum never wakes up until *Oprah* starts so I can, like, stay in the house anyway until, like, um, err, what's that thing what comes after two?'

'Three.'

'Yeah, I can like stay in the house until three o'clock and my mum wouldn't know.'

'We didn't get the witch girl, though,' said friend one.

'Yeah, well, I decided to let her off. She's well scared and won't bother me again,' said Bridie.

'Yeah, but listen,' said friend two, 'what about the sack I took to school? My dad only got it last week. He'll go totally spazz if I don't take it back.'

'Well, just tell him you brought it to school for, like, show and tell, and that nerdy girl stole it.'

'Cool,' said friend two. 'Anyway, I think my dad's got loads of other sacks. He's always coming in and telling my mum he's got another one.'

'Whatever.'

6

So because of Betty's magic Mr and Mrs Hulbert never found out about the trouble at school, which was a good thing because they probably would have moved house again and they didn't want to.

Mrs Hulbert was over the moon that Ffiona had her first best friend, but she also thought that maybe Mordonna could become *her* first best friend. At that point she hadn't met Nerlin, but she wondered if maybe he might become Mr Hulbert's first ever best friend too.

And maybe, she thought, *Betty has a little brother who could be Claude's friend.*

She decided to ask the whole Flood family over for afternoon tea, but first she had to go to the library and get out a book to find out exactly what afternoon teas were. She had heard about them, but had never had one or been to one or even seen one on television, because the Hulberts didn't have a television, though she had heard a play on the radio once where everyone had had afternoon tea and it had sounded quite nice with lots of tinkling tea cups and cucumber sandwiches.

Mrs Hulbert had bought her first cucumber earlier that week. She had always thought they were a bit too exotic for the likes of her family and buying it had made her feel quite daring. She hadn't actually eaten any of it or told Mr Hulbert about it, but every morning she looked at it sitting in the fridge and felt her life was about to get a lot more exciting.

'There's probably a magazine about them,' Mr Hulbert suggested. 'Something like *Afternoon Teas Weekly*.'

But before she could get herself down to the

newsagents or the library, Mordonna came over to the Hulberts' house and invited them over for a barbie the next Sunday.

'Well, that's sorted that out, then,' Mr Hulbert said. 'We'll find out all about afternoon tea and then we'll know exactly what to do when we ask them back.'

'Yes,' said Mrs Hulbert. 'But I don't understand about the barbie. Does she mean Ffiona is supposed to take her doll?'

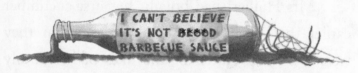

'I suppose we'd better have cucumber sandwiches,' said Mordonna. 'They'd be the sort of thing refined people like the Hulberts would expect.'

'The Hulberts aren't posh, Mum,' said Betty. 'They're just ordinary people like us.'

'Sweetheart, how many times do I have to remind you?' said Mordonna. 'Nobody is like us.'

'No, I know, Mum,' said Betty. 'What I mean is, they're not stuck up at all. They're nice, normal people.'

'Yes, darling, and nice, normal people eat cucumber sandwiches for afternoon tea,' said Mordonna. 'I've seen it on the Lifestyle Channel. They have white pepper and the crusts cut off.'

'So no bat kebabs or rat rissoles then,' said Nerlin, who was sitting at the kitchen table sharpening his skewers.

'I don't think so, but you'd better check in the book, darling.'

The book which Mordonna was referring to was probably the most useful book a wizard or witch can have when they are trying to live as unobtrusively as possible in the so-called 'normal' human world.

Grandma Floode's Book of Ye Handy Hintes

The first edition was written in 1683 by one of Nerlin's relatives and was called Grandma Floode's Book of Ye Handy Hintes. Since then the 'e's and 'ye' have been dropped so the current edition of the book is called Granny Flood's Book of Handy Hints. There have been suggestions that it should be called something cooler and more modern like Humans for Dummies, but most readers agree the title it has is nice and comforting, which is exactly what wizards and witches need when trying to deal with the weird and frightening world of humans.

The book has tons of information on things that wizards find perfectly OK that simply freak humans out. For example, humans get really distressed if they buy a sandwich, take a big bite and then find a long black hair in it. They even get upset if it turns out to be one of their own hairs. But wizards, on the other hand, quite often will add hairs to their meals to enhance the eating experience. In wizardy countries like

Transylvania Waters you can buy packets of hairs specially for putting in food, and there is quite an industry surrounding the whole thing, including a monthly magazine called What Hair,[19] *hair-flavoured crisps and a* Hair of the Month Club. *The hair generally agreed to be the very best for food enhancement is from the almost extinct Pocket Vampire Bat. Only the whiskers from its left ear are used and as each bat only has seven whiskers in its left ear,[20] they are staggeringly expensive. It is said that to eat something with one of these hairs in it is like dying and being carried up to heaven by an angel made entirely of milk chocolate who sings to you in a voice sweeter than condensed milk. Some claim the nasal hairs from the legendary Himalayan Yeti are even better, though most people don't believe yetis exist, and no one*

---

[19] *In the back of this book you will find a page from* What Hair.
[20] *They have no whiskers in their right ears because they sleep with that ear to the wall.*

actually knows anyone who had eaten one of these hairs, but lots of people know someone who claims they know someone who knows someone who had a friend who . . .

The part of the book Mordonna was referring to was the Equivalents section, where you look up the wizard food and it gives you the human equivalent.

'Bat kebabs, bat kebabs,' said Nerlin, flicking through the pages. 'Amazing. It says cucumber sandwiches with white pepper and the crusts cut off.'

'See, I told you,' said Mordonna. 'What about the rat rissoles? What's the human equivalent of them?'

'Ratatouille.'

'Oh.'

'Yes,' said Nerlin, 'and it sounds dreadful. It's got absolutely no rat in it at all, just those horrible vegetable things.'

'Well, I've said it before and I'll say it again,' said Mordonna, 'humans are weird.'

'These cucumber sandwiches?' said Betty. 'Won't they taste odd cooked on the barbie?'

'Not according to the book,' said Nerlin. 'That's what you do, spray them with oil, cook them on the barbie and then cover them with tomato sauce.'[21]

'Right. Morbid, you go down to the petrol station and get a litre of oil,' said Mordonna. 'And Betty, see if you can find if we've got the human sort of tomato sauce stuff, not the one with blood in that your granny likes.'

After reading the book some more, Mordonna made cucumber sandwiches, which she had to throw away after Betty said she didn't think the Hulberts would enjoy sandwiches cut out in the shape of human skulls. She then made a second

---

[21] *Although the book was a bestseller in the world of wizards, large bits of it were completely useless because some of the authors had never actually lived among humans or done any proper research.*

SANDWITCHES

batch and cut them into squares, which everyone agreed was nowhere near as attractive. Nerlin put on a face mask and some rubber gloves and cut up a whole lot of vegetables, which Betty cooked into ratatouille. She had to do this blindfolded to resist the almost uncontrollable desire to add bits of rat.

'But a few dried tails would make the whole thing taste so much better,' she kept saying, and everyone agreed.

'I know, I know,' Mordonna said. 'Nevertheless, we won't put them in.'

'Well, what about a few hairs?' Betty suggested. 'Just mild ones like rabbit.'

'No.'

The twins were beside themselves – which meant there were four of them – at the thought of Ffiona being at their house for a whole afternoon. They made a huge tray of cakes in all sorts of strange shapes and colours, some of which were very rude – especially the ones that looked exactly like human . Satanella spent all of Saturday practising not biting anyone, while Merlinmary charged up the garden lights. Even Valla, who was at work at the Blood Bank all day, made some bright red decorations to hang in the trees. They looked remarkably like red blood corpuscles, but Mordonna guessed that the Hulberts probably didn't know what blood cells looked like so she didn't make him change them.

'If they ask, we'll say they are the national emblem of Transylvania Waters,' she said.

'They are,' said Valla.

The only thing they still needed was a barbecue, so Nerlin and Winchflat went down to one of the cellars and made one. Considering neither of them actually knew what a barbecue looked like, this was quite an achievement, but hey, wizards can do that sort of stuff.

Sunday arrived with wind, clouds and rain, but Winchflat went down to his cellar, twiddled a few knobs on his 'Perpetual Sunshine Machine' and all the wind shrivelled up and vanished while the clouds went off to annoy Belgium. He adjusted the temperature gauge and the air grew comfortably warm. Merlinmary breathed flames onto some fallen branches and made charcoal for the barbecue.

'Now, I want everyone to be on their best behaviour,' said Mordonna. 'The Hulberts are shy sort of people so I don't want to see any body parts being dragged round the garden. If you do play

catch or fetch with the children, Satanella, do it with a red rubber ball, not a knotted ball of pig's intestines.'

Along the road, Mrs Hulbert was giving her family similar instructions. 'Now, I want everyone to be on their best behaviour,' she said. 'The Floods are not like other people, but Mrs Flood and Betty have been very nice so I'm sure the rest of the family will be too. And remember, they are the only family that has come and said hello to us since we moved in.'

This bird was flying by when it saw the Hulberts and fell asleep from boredom.

'Don't worry, they're all nice, Mum,' said Ffiona. 'They might look a bit weird – well, actually, some of them look very weird indeed – but they are really nice.'

This was said for the benefit of Mr Hulbert, who was very, very, very, very normal and tended to get quite nervous when he came into contact with anything that was the slightest bit out of the ordinary. A car painted in fluorescent pink with blue spots on the doors passed him once and it upset him for a week. Mrs Hulbert ironed all the folds

out of the newspaper every morning so he wouldn't worry about missing any words in the creases.

Ffiona's little brother, Claude, was young enough to think everything was exciting. He had only learned to walk a few months earlier – though he was still much better at falling over than standing up. He was also just starting to speak words that made sense, and now had a vocabulary that included the words goo, poo, and Ffuffuff, which is what he called Ffiona, and ughherr, which was what he called everyone else. He was still much too young to have caught his parents' anxiety.

'I don't suppose Betty's got a younger brother or sister who could play with Claude, has she?' said Mrs Hulbert as they walked down the road.

'No, Betty's the youngest,' said Ffiona.

'Oh well.'

But Mrs Hulbert needn't have worried. As the Floods front gate opened itself to let the Hulberts in, a lot of things happened at once. Firstly, Mordonna released a mega squirt of relaxing-with-witches

powder into the air, making sure a good shot of it went up Mr Hulbert's nose.

Secondly, Claude saw Satanella and went racing towards her, with Mrs Hulbert trying to rescue him. As he reached Satanella, the toddler tripped on the path and fell over, but instead of crashing down on the concrete and hurting himself, he landed on a nice soft dog as Satanella threw herself underneath him.

'Goo, poo, ffuffuff, ughherr,' he chuckled as he buried his face in Satanella's fur.

'Goo, poo, ffuffuff, Satanella,' said Satanella, licking Claude's face.

'Wow, I've never licked a baby human before,' she added. 'Of course, I've always wanted to. Who hasn't? And now I have, they taste even nicer than I imagined, a sort of mixture of stewed prunes and earth.'

'That's what he was eating before we came here,' said Ffiona.

'D-d . . . d-d . . . did that dog, um, err, speak?' said Mrs Hulbert.

Mr Hulbert just stood open-mouthed. There was nothing in his brain that said what you're supposed to do when you hear a dog talk, so all he could do was stare.

'Let me explain,' said Mordonna, putting her arm round Mrs Hulbert's shoulder and taking her into the house.

'Let me explain,' said Nerlin, putting his arm round Mr Hulbert's shoulder and walking him down the back garden to his shed.

'I think that went well,' said Betty.

'Compared to what?' said Ffiona and the two girls burst out laughing.

When they heard Ffiona laugh, Morbid and Silent were so overcome with love and blushes that they had to run and hide in their room.

'I wonder if she will ever marry me,' Morbid said to himself as they looked down into the garden where the two girls were playing with Claude and Satanella.

How can she? Silent said inside his twin's head. *She's going to marry me.*

Now in the human world this sort of situation would lead to terrible fights and possibly even murder, but wizards are a lot more intelligent than humans and can usually find much more civilised solutions to their problems, solutions that generally avoid killing each other, though sometimes someone might get turned into a toad.

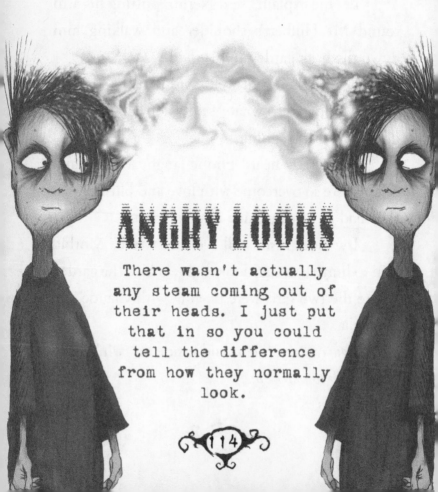

ANGRY LOOKS

There wasn't actually any steam coming out of their heads. I just put that in so you could tell the difference from how they normally look.

'When we are old enough to get married,' said Morbid, 'we'll get Winchflat to photocopy Ffiona so we can both marry her.'

Just so long as we make sure that neither of us ever finds out which is the original and which the copy, Silent telepathed. *Agreed?*

'Agreed,' said Morbid.

The twins squeezed the insides out of a Giant Transylvanian Slime Worm and wiped it on each other's faces, which is the wizard version of spitting on your palm and shaking hands.

'Maybe we could get him to make three photocopies,' said Morbid. 'Then we could have a spare Ffiona each.'

I don't think he'd do that, said Silent.

The twins realised that if they did marry two Ffionas, it would be the end of being wizards, not for them, but for any children that they might have. Because it is a well-known fact that if a wizard or witch marries someone who is not a wizard or witch, none of their children will be able to do any magic at all. There was a rumour a few years ago

that a taxi driver who had a witch for a mother but an ordinary human for a father could do magic, but it was all a misunderstanding. The Magic Examiners came and told him to turn his taxi into something.

'No problem, mate,' he said.

He grabbed hold of the steering wheel and turned it into a side street.

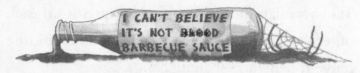

I CAN'T BELIEVE
IT'S NOT BLOOD
BARBECUE SAUCE

Sitting at the table in the Floods kitchen with what appeared to be completely normal human cups of tea, Mordonna explained to Mrs Hulbert that Satanella wasn't really a dog but her daughter, who had been changed into a dog by accident.[22]

'So there's nothing weird to get worried about,' she said. 'Satanella isn't a talking dog at all, she's a little girl.'

'Oh, umm, right,' said Mrs Hulbert.

---

[22] *See* The Floods 3: Home & Away.

'Though when I was a girl, my grandmother had a whippet that could recite its nine times table up to nine times six,' Mordonna added, 'but that's not really the same thing.'

'No, yes, umm, I see,' said Mrs Hulbert.

The inside of her head was very confused. On the one hand, Mordonna was the only person in Acacia Avenue who had been friendly since they had moved there. On the other hand, her new friend had a small talking dog that she said was her daughter. But if Mrs Hulbert's parents had taught her one useful thing,[23] it was that you should never judge a book by its cover. The Floods might look weird, but they were kind and friendly and since Ffiona had met Betty, she had been happier than ever before. So Mrs Hulbert decided that if Mordonna said the little dog was her daughter, she would believe her.

---

[23] *They had actually taught her two things. The second one was a rather nice recipe for upside-down cake, which she had never made because an upside-down cake seemed too much like showing off.*

Through the window, Mrs Hulbert could see Claude tottering around the garden after Satanella, who was tossing a big red rubber ball up in the air. He was grinning and laughing and waving his little arms around in total happiness. And every time he tripped over his feet, which he did every ten steps or so, Satanella always managed to throw herself underneath him to cushion his fall. As Mrs Hulbert watched, Claude and Satanella landed on top of a flower-covered mound near the clothesline. The ground parted slightly and a skeleton arm came up out of the earth. It patted Claude gently on the head, ran its fingers through Satanella's fur and vanished back into the ground.

Don't panic, said the cautious voice that lives inside the head of all slightly nervous people like Mrs Hulbert.

'Don't panic,' said Mordonna. 'That's just my mother saying hello. Nothing to worry about, she adores little children.'

'Right, OK, lovely.'

'More tea?' said Mordonna. 'I wonder what

the boys are up to. It's probably time we should be lighting the barbie.'

'I don't think Ffiona brought her Barbie with her,' said Mrs Hulbert.

'It's not the doll, Mummy,' said Ffiona as she and Betty came into the kitchen. 'Mrs Flood means the barbecue.'

Meanwhile, Nerlin had taken Mr Hulbert to the shed at the bottom of the garden because he'd seen on TV that the shed was where blokes went to do blokey things. Nerlin hadn't built this shed. It had belonged to the previous owners of number 11, the Dents,[24] and it was full of all the usual things that human men have in sheds: a couple of very grubby worn-out armchairs complete with mouse nests in the stuffing, a rusty fridge, dozens of broken household items like old toasters and video machines, and lots and lots of tools. There was everything from screwdrivers and angle grinders right up to a huge electric welder.

Nerlin was hoping Mr Hulbert could explain what all these things were for. Unfortunately, Mr Hulbert was not a shed type of man either. He was more a stamp-collecting man.

Nerlin didn't want to admit he knew nothing about all the stuff, so he decided to bluff.

'So how about this then, eh?' he said, taking

---

[24] *See* The Floods 1: Neighbours.

a bright yellow electric chainsaw off a shelf.

'Very nice,' said Mr Hulbert, who also didn't want to admit he hadn't the faintest idea what the thing was. 'It looks very powerful.'

'I should say so,' said Nerlin, and pulled the starting cord.[25]

The chainsaw roared into life with such a loud scream that Nerlin dropped it. Unless you are in zero gravity, which neither Nerlin nor the chainsaw were, when you drop things they tend to fall downwards. And downwards was where Nerlin's feet lived.

The chainsaw flapped around for a bit and then stopped. The reason it stopped was because it was jammed, and what it was jammed on was Nerlin's ankle.

'Oops,' said Nerlin. He picked up his foot, which was now sitting under the workbench.

Mr Hulbert fainted.

---

[25] *You should NEVER use power tools at all except under adult supervision, and only then if the adult is not Belgian or less than fifty centimetres tall.*

'It's all right,' said Nerlin. 'It's only one foot. I've got another one.'

Mr Hulbert said nothing on account of still being in a just-fainted situation. Nerlin picked him up and sat him in one of the old armchairs. Instinctively, even though two minutes ago he hadn't known what an electric drill was, he plugged

a drill in, stuck a paintbrush in the chuck and turned it on. The bristles spun round, creating a draft of fresh air, which brought Mr Hulbert round.

'Shouldn't we call an ambulance?' he spluttered.

'No, you'll be all right,' said Nerlin. 'Just take a few deep breaths.'

'No, I mean your foot, er, all the blood . . .' Mr Hulbert began as he felt himself going faint again.

'No, it's fine, I'm a wizard,' said Nerlin and began mumbling a spell to himself. 'See,' he said as his foot re-joined itself to his body.

'But, but,' said Mr Hulbert, 'shouldn't it be on the end of your leg? It looks funny on top of your head.'

'Just kidding,' said Nerlin, wiggling his toes.

Mr Hulbert looked green.

Poor bugger, Nerlin thought. *Humans have no sense of humour.*

'Here, this'll make you laugh,' he said and he

twisted his foot round and poked his big toe up his nose.

It didn't make Mr Hulbert laugh. It made him faint again.

Nerlin fixed his foot back in the right place, got rid of all the blood and woke Mr Hulbert up again.

As he came round, Nerlin explained to him that the Floods were not like ordinary people. This was a very good time to tell someone as normal as Mr Hulbert something as big as this because fainting had made him very light-headed and ideas that might have frightened him at other times just slipped into his head now without a problem.

'A wizard?' he said. 'You're all wizards?'

'Yes,' said Nerlin.

'Gosh,' said Mr Hulbert. 'I know a wizard.'

He was about to say, 'Just wait until I tell all my friends,' when he realised he didn't actually have any friends apart from Mrs Hulbert, Ffiona and baby Claude, and they probably knew already.

'So the elephant thing with my Ffiona really did happen?' he said.

'Absolutely,' said Nerlin. 'With my Betty as her friend, she need never worry about being bullied again.'

'And all this stuff?' Mr Hulbert asked, waving his arms round the shed. 'Is this special wizard equipment?'

'No, it's all human stuff,' said Nerlin. 'I was kind of hoping you could tell *me* what it's all used for.'

''Fraid not,' said Mr Hulbert. 'Though I think that thing there is a hammer and that might be a screwdriver.'

'What do you do with them?' said Nerlin.

'I haven't the faintest idea,' said Mr Hulbert. 'I do know one thing, though. They've got nothing to do with stamp collecting.'

'I suppose we better go and start the barbie,' said Nerlin, whose entire barbecue knowledge consisted of two facts: it's something blokes do, and it involves fire.

'Yes,' said Mr Hulbert, who knew slightly less about barbies than Nerlin.

'We must do this again,' said Nerlin as they left the shed.

'Except maybe without the foot chopping off,' said Mr Hulbert.

'Yes,' Nerlin agreed. 'I've ruined a perfectly good sock.'

Mordonna and Mrs Hulbert were already doing the barbecue when their husbands got there. They were only too happy to let their husbands take over and went off to sit in the shade, although Mordonna wasn't too happy about letting her husband near open flames because, ever since she had known him, Nerlin had always shown an unhealthy interest in news items that involved setting fire to things such as old ladies and big forests. If she had heard of the word 'pyromaniac' she would have thought Nerlin would make a very good one.

Nerlin flicked his cloak over his shoulder. Mr Hulbert took off his tie, and the two of them began poking things about with a pair of tongs and a poker.

'Those two seem to be getting on like, er . . .' Mordonna began. She was about to say 'like a house on fire', but thought it was probably tempting fate.

'They do, don't they,' Mrs Hulbert agreed. 'My Lionel is dreadfully shy normally, and I must say, I never thought I'd see the day when he would

be seen in public without his tie on. It's quite exciting.'

Exciting is different for everyone. Some people can only get excited by jumping out of a plane above Niagara Falls standing on a surfboard with a paper bag over their heads and one arm tied behind someone else's back. Other people like to ride horses across wide open plains towards golden sunsets and yet others like to boldly go where no one has gone before to discover wonderful new worlds, plants and fishes and frogs.

And then there are people like the Hulberts.

Mr Hulbert could find excitement in a new box of stamp hinges and Mrs Hulbert felt her heart go all of a flutter when she saw her husband standing on the other side of the Floods' lawn without his tie on and the smoke from the barbecue wafting around him, making him look, to his wife's timid imagination, a little bit like a primeval caveman.

'It makes him look ten years younger,' she said and undid the top button of her blouse.

This was not particularly wicked as she had fifteen other buttons – nineteen if you included the cuffs[26] – that were still firmly done up, but it was enough to make Mr Hulbert's pulse race when he glanced across and saw her.

'This food's taking ages to cook,' said Nerlin. 'Think I'll go and have a look in my shed for something to put on the fire.'

Ancient inherited memories of his ancestors dancing naked with no clothes on while they set large parts of Belgium on fire stirred deep in Nerlin's soul as he scoured the shed for some seriously dangerous accelerants. And finally he saw it: a big bright red can with a danger sign on the side, and the word 'Petrol'.

'That'll get the cucumber sandwiches crispy,' he said as he ran back across the lawn.

His mother-in-law, Queen Scratchrot, woke up in her coffin by the clothesline. She stretched her arms and her left hand poked up out of the

---

[26] *Twenty-three if you counted the two pockets as well, and twenty-five if you added the two spare ones sewn inside the hem.*

lawn at the precise moment that Nerlin's right foot passed by.

He flew through the air, the petrol can flying ahead of him in a dead straight line towards the barbecue. Of course the top came off the can too, otherwise this would be a lot more boring.

So instead of a small egg-cupful of petrol on the fire to help things along a bit, seven litres splashed everywhere and there was a very big explosion.

This is what happened to the various people in the garden.

Baby Claude Hulbert shot up into the air and landed in a tree, followed by Satanella. After Satanella had helped him down he began to cry because he wanted to do it again.

Queen Scratchrot got a burning cinder down the feeding tube Mordonna poured her rat-tail soup into. Not realising the cinder wasn't her dinner, the Queen ate it and asked for seconds.

Mordonna and Mrs Hulbert both had to go inside and brush the ash out of their hair.

Mrs Hulbert also had to pick three slices of hot cucumber out of her blouse.[27]

Valla had to rush up to his room and give himself a fresh coat of white paint to cover the soot stains.

Merlimary blew a fuse, but fortunately the fuse was in the local powerstation so it didn't do her any harm.

Twelve cockroaches who had just moved into a nice tin can that had rolled under the barbecue were totally fried.

Betty and Ffiona were unharmed as they had been inside in the kitchen eating Zabaglione ice-cream.[28]

All the food got totally wrecked, which was probably a good thing considering they were cooking it in engine oil instead of vegetable oil.

---

[27] *This made her wonder if undoing her top button had been such a good idea after all.*

[28] *And now I've written that, I'll have to go into my kitchen and eat some too. By the way, if you're ever in Bellingen make sure you go to the Gelato Bar and get some too because it is brilliant.*

And last, but the opposite of least, Nerlin and Mr Hulbert took the full force of the sausage explosion.[29] They were thrown across the garden in a shower of burnt meat and fried onions and landed in a dazed but delicious-smelling heap by the back door.

'Oops,' said Nerlin.

'Are we dead?' said Mr Hulbert. 'Have we gone to heaven? It smells like heaven except there's no tomato sauce.'

Betty and Ffiona rushed out of the kitchen and helped their dazed dads to their feet.

'I think I'd like to lie down,' said Nerlin and lay down.

'Why is the world spinning round like that?' said Mr Hulbert and fell over on top of him.

'Why don't you both go and lie down in the . . . umm, err, nice cool relaxy place downstairs

---

[29] *The cucumber sandwiches, being a lot lighter, had shot up over their heads, and missed them. One even got caught up in a cloud and was later rained down onto a very confused postman in a small Hebridean village.*

with the nice soft relaxy beds?' said Betty. 'Come on.'

What she meant to say was, 'Why don't you both go and lie down in Valla's special mortuary in two of his lovely padded coffins,' but she realised that the idea of lying in an open coffin in a dark room might scare the living daylights out of someone like Mr Hulbert.

'You know, Father, Valla's special room,' she said. She took the two men down to the cellar, tucked them up in two coffins with a couple of shrouds to keep them warm and turned out the light.

'There you are. Have a nice peaceful rest,' she said and went back upstairs.

There were four other coffins in the darkened cellar and one of them was already occupied. Neither the two dads nor their daughters realised this.

With the two husbands out of the way, the two mothers cooked a new batch of sausages and cucumber sandwiches on the barbie and got on like a house on fire, which is a stupid expression because it means they were both either burnt to the ground, or drenched from head to foot with a fire hose. Neither of these two things happened to them, though the first one did happen to the barbecue when the cucumber sandwiches caught fire because Mordonna had used engine oil on some of them when she had run out of butter.

'I kept telling Dad you don't make barbecues

out of wood,' said Winchflat, 'but he said it looked so much nicer than metal.'

'Oh well,' said Mordonna, poking around in the ashes to see if any of the sausages had survived, 'we've still got the cucumber sandwiches.'

They went back indoors and ate the sandwiches, which Mordonna and her children thought were a bit lifeless, but Mrs Hulbert thought were very sophisticated because she'd never had sandwiches with the crusts cut off before.

'It's a wicked waste of food,' her mother had always told her. 'And as everyone knows, crusts are really good for you.'

No one knows why crusts are supposedly good for you, and in actual fact it's one of the seventeen billion old wives' tales that mothers have made up over the centuries to make their children do things they don't want to. The truth is that the only good thing about crusts is the word itself. It's one the wizard world's favourite words, because it makes you think of crispy scabs with edges that

*beg you to stick your fingernail underneath them
and peel them off, and picking scabs is number
three in the wizard's top ten of brilliant things
to do.*[30]

Mordonna had sprinkled some of her relaxing-with-witches powder in the tea and the cucumber sandwiches and now Mrs Hulbert was feeling more relaxed than she had done since she had been three days old and fast asleep.

'Would you like me to make an upside-down cake?' Mrs Hulbert said. 'Seeing as how the sausages were ruined.'

'That would be nice,' said Mordonna. 'I haven't made one of those since I was a girl. I'd forgotten all about them . . . hooking your feet over the beam in the castle kitchen and hanging upside down over the table with your wand between your teeth and trying to stop your skirt falling up over your face.'

---

[30] *I cannot tell you what numbers one and two on the list are
because they are just too gross to write down.*

'I don't think my mother's recipe is quite the same as that . . .' Mrs Hulbert began, but Mordonna was already collecting bowls and spoons.

She flashed her wand at the ceiling and a large wooden beam appeared, stretching from one end of the kitchen to the other.

'OK,' she said, 'tuck your skirt into your knickers, you can go first. I'll give you a lift up and make sure you don't fall into the mixing bowl.'

'I, umm, no, I, err . . .'

'Go on, Mum,' said Ffiona.

'Oh, what the flip,' said Mrs Hulbert.[31]

She tucked her skirt into her thick navy blue undies and climbed up onto the table. Mordonna grabbed her round the waist, flipped her upside down and hooked her feet over the beam.

'Here, you can use my Cooking Wand,' said Mordonna. 'Start stirring and I'll conjure up the ingredients.'

---

[31] *What Mrs Hulbert was thinking was, 'What the hell', but she had never said the 'H' word before and although she was feeling very relaxed, she wasn't quite ready to go that far.*

She picked up her Shopping Wand and began waving it in the air. A bag of flour appeared from nowhere and poured itself into the bowl. Six very confused chickens suddenly materialised on the draining board and laid six eggs, which cracked themselves into the bowl.

'Not so fast, dinner,' Mordonna blurted out as the chickens began to disappear.

In a flash of an eye and far too quick to be painful, four of the chickens plucked themselves and jumped into the freezer as more ingredients decided they had spent too long on the shelves of the local supermarket.

Hanging from the beam, Mrs Hulbert felt the blood rushing to her head. As she spun the wand round in the mixing bowl, the room began to spin too and she felt her feet losing their grip on the beam. Finally she could hold on no longer and went crashing down into huge mixing bowl. As she did, Mordonna did the special upside-down cake twist with her wand and Mrs Hulbert ended sitting

the right way up right in the middle of the cake mixture.

'Perfect cake-flip,' said Mordonna. 'I've never seen a first-timer do it so well.'

Mrs Hulbert sat with the cake mix oozing into all her nooks and crannies, not quite sure what to think. When she'd got up that morning, she'd been a bit apprehensive about visiting the Floods. She had thought they might be offered weird things to eat or be asked to wear pointy witch hats. One of the millions of things she hadn't thought of was that she might end up sitting with her bottom in a huge bowl of cake mix. If someone had told her this was a possibility, she would have stayed at home and had to lie down in a dark room with a wet hankie on her forehead.

But now, she was amazed to find that she had a huge grin on her face. She felt as if a door had opened and she had walked out of her grey home into a world full of bright colours where anything was possible.

'What do we do now?' she asked.

'Well, you go upstairs and have a shower while I put the cake in the oven,' said Mordonna. As Mrs Hulbert stepped down onto the floor, where Claude and Satanella were licking as much cake mixture off her legs as they could reach, Mordonna added, 'How many socks were you wearing, one or two?'

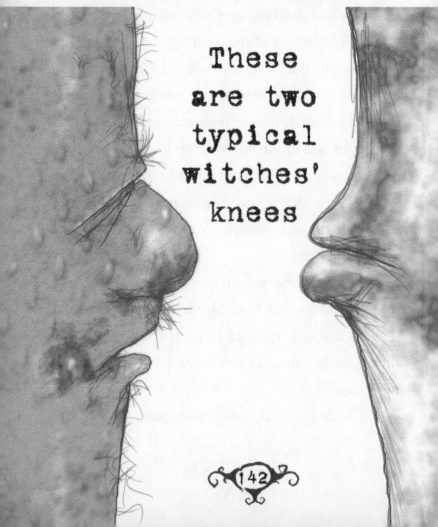

These are two typical witches' knees

'Two,' said Mrs Hulbert.

'Oh well, too late now,' said Mordonna. 'It can be like a lucky rat's foot in a Christmas pudding.[32] Whoever finds it will get a prize.'

After her shower Mrs Hulbert came downstairs in one of Mordonna's dresses that was rather revealing, but she was in the sort of mood where she felt quite excited by it. No one apart from Mr Hulbert had ever seen her knees before, and Mr Hulbert had only seen them on special occasions like his birthday.

'Don't you have lovely knees,' said Mordonna. 'Mine are all bony. I wish they were like yours.'

'But if you can do magic,' said Mrs Hulbert, 'can't you change your knees to be exactly how you want them?'

'I suppose I could, but Nerlin loves my knees as they are,' Mordonna explained. 'He says they remind him of the day we met. I fell down a hole,

---

[32] *Humans usually use an old-fashioned sixpence, which is far more dangerous. At least if you swallow a rat's foot, it tastes nice and won't choke you like a small coin could.*

you know, and landed right on top of him. He had two bruises from my knees right in the middle of his back for weeks.'

'Mum, do you think me and Ffiona should go and wake our dads up?' said Betty.

'No, it's nice and peaceful,' said Mordonna. 'We'll just let them sleep.'

Which would have been fine except that the thing that had been sleeping in the other occupied coffin had just woken up. It was Winchflat's latest invention, the thing that he had been secretly creating for the past fortnight.

Winchflat Flood had developed a taste for old-fashioned movies and his favourite was *Frankenstein*. He particularly liked the scenes where the mad doctor created a living creature out of a pile of bits from dead people, including a crazy murderer.

The trouble was, Winchflat didn't realise the movie was a made-up story. He thought it was a documentary and that it had all really happened. Humans would realise it wasn't true straight away, but Winchflat was a wizard and his father had

told him stories about growing up in Transylvania Waters, where it was not that unusual to make new people out of the bits of dead ones. There were even specialist upmarket mad doctors who would create creatures to order, and Winchflat's grandfather King Quatorze had had a servant made with three heads all programmed to tell him how wonderful he was.

So naturally, having seen the *Frankenstein* movie, it was obvious that Winchflat would want to create a living-dead playmate of his own. This is what was sleeping in the other coffin:

Igorina was mostly male apart from the bits that weren't. The bits that weren't were mostly female apart from the bits that weren't. The other bits were an assortment of Lego, wire, string and cardboard. Winchflat had searched through the rubbish bins behind the undertakers to see if there were any old body parts there, but all he found was a finger. It

wasn't until he was leaving that he realised he'd been searching in the burger bar's rubbish bin.

'You have simply no idea how difficult it is to get bits of dead body in this town,' Winchflat explained later. 'I mean, humans are so wasteful. You go to a funeral parlour or a hospital and ask for a simple thing like an arm and they freak out. The ridiculous thing is that they would rather burn them or bury them in the ground than use them again. It's such a waste.'

Winchflat knew that very few girls are attracted to skinny green-skinned boys with dead eyes, even if they do have enormous feet – unless, of course, they are Goth girls, and he didn't like Goths. They looked just too healthy. So he realised he was very unlikely to get a proper girlfriend, and might have end up marrying Igorina. Because of this he thought of Igorina as a girl even though she was less than twenty percent female.

After he had created her in his special secret laboratory, Winchflat had carried Igorina down to his coffin cellar to sleep.

Now she had woken up.

'AAHHHHHHHH,' she groaned and then, 'UURRRGGGHHHHH.'

'What?' said Nerlin.

'Eh?' said Mr Hulbert. 'What did you say?'

'I didn't say anything. I thought it was you,' said Nerlin.

'OOOOOHHHHHHH.'

'Who's there?'

Most wizards, even ones like Nerlin who weren't much good at magic, can rub their fingers together like two sticks and make them glow in the dark. Nerlin held up his hands and there was Igorina sitting up in her coffin.

'Dada,' she said, looking at Nerlin and grinning.

Mr Hulbert took one look at Igorina's face and screamed.

'Dada,' she said, looking at Mr Hulbert and grinning as widely as she could.

This was a bad move.

Her jaw fell off.

Mr Hulbert fainted. Nerlin, who was used to that sort of thing, climbed out of his coffin, picked the jaw up and pushed it back into place. Igorina touched him gently on the cheek.

'There's a good boy, er, girl, er, umm . . .' said Nerlin. 'You stay there.'

He picked up the unconscious Mr Hulbert and carried him out into the tunnel, making sure to shut the door and close the three massive bolts on the outside of the door. Just to be on the safe side he turned the key in the lock and jammed a wooden chair under the handle.

'He needs a forgetting spell,' he whispered to Mordonna as he lay Mr Hulbert on the couch. 'Where's Winchflat?'

Mordonna put a damp towel over Mr Hulbert's

face and muttered a few words. The poor man came round with all memories of Igorina wiped from his brain.

'Ooh, my head,' he said.

'Poor darling,' said Mrs Hulbert. 'Maybe Mordonna can do a little magic and take your nasty headache away.'

'Absolutely,' said Mordonna and gave him an aspirin.

'I can see your knees,' Mr Hulbert whispered to his wife. 'I'd forgotten how nice they were.'

'Mmmm,' she said, blushing as if she was a teenager again. 'And you aren't wearing your tie.'

'Oh no, sorry, dear.'

'I think maybe it's time for a change,' said Mrs Hulbert. 'Time to let our hair down a bit.'

'I haven't got any to let down,' said Mr Hulbert.

'But I have,' said Mrs Hulbert and pulled out the twenty-four hair pins that had held her hair back for so long they had begun to go rusty.

Her long brown hair tumbled down all over

150

Mr Hulbert's face. It was the first time in the fifteen years since he had met his wife that he had ever seen her hair out. Her hair was long and shining and beautiful and it smelled of roses, and as it fell over her husband's face three brilliant butterflies flew out of it. Mr Hulbert began to smile, not the shy awkward smile he usually did, but the big proper smile he hadn't done since he had been five years old.

Then he fainted again.

'I think it's time I took him home,' said Mrs Hulbert when her husband came round again.

'Why doesn't Ffiona stay for a sleepover?' Mordonna suggested.

Mrs Hulbert did her best to hide her excitement. Other people's children had sleepovers. She'd read about them in magazines, but no one had ever asked Ffiona to go on one before. Of course it meant that Ffiona would want to ask Betty back for a sleepover at their house and that would mean at least a week getting the house really, really spotless and probably even having to buy a new toilet seat and painting the inside of the cupboard under the stairs, but it would be worth it, for Ffiona's sake.

So Mr and Mrs Hulbert and Claude went home. As they left the Floods' house, Mr Hulbert said, 'You know what, I think maybe it's time we got a television.'

'Winchflat, get down here this minute!' Mordonna shouted up the stairs.

'What's the matter?' said Winchflat.

'The thing down in the cellar,' said Mordonna. 'The thing in the coffin. I think you better explain yourself.'

'Oh, you mean Igorina. It's nothing to worry about,' said Winchflat.

'Nothing to worry about? Nothing to worry about!' said Mordonna. 'What is it? I mean, who is it? I mean, where did it come from?'

'It's just Igorina,' Winchflat explained. 'I made

her, like in the *Frankenstein* movies.'

'What, you mean with a bolt through her neck and the brain out of a psychotic murderer?'

'No, of course not,' said Winchflat. 'Where would I get a brain out of a psychotic murderer? This isn't Transylvania Waters, you know. You can't just go into a brain shop and buy one. No, it's an ordinary human brain. I sort of borrowed it.'

'Borrowed it?' said Mordonna suspiciously.

'I got it out of an accountant while he was asleep,' said Winchflat. 'No one will miss it.'

'Well, I imagine the accountant will.'

'I doubt it,' said Winchflat. 'Have you ever met an accountant?'

'Well, I think you'd better dismantle it and put all the bits back where you got them from.'

'But . . . but . . . that would be murder,' said Winchflat. 'And besides, she's my new best friend. I mean, Betty's just got one and so have you and Satanella and even dad's got Mr Hulbert as a sort of friend. So I want one.'

'The twins haven't got new best friends and

neither have Valla or Merlinmary, so you're not the only one.'

'The twins have had new best friends ever since they were born. They've got each other,' said Winchflat. 'And Merlinmary's got the national grid and Valla's got a whole room full of blood corpuscles. I haven't got anyone.'

'He does have a point,' said Nerlin.

So it was agreed that Winchflat could keep Igorina, but he had to look after her properly and clean her cage out every day and exercise her regularly.

'Though of course, you must never take her out in daylight,' said Nerlin.

'Probably not before midnight, actually,' said Mordonna.

'Can we see her?' asked Ffiona.

So they all went down to the coffin cellar. It was exactly as Nerlin had left it. Winchflat turned the key, pulled the chair out from under the door handle and slid back the three massive bolts.

The room was empty.

Winchflat turned on the light and looked in each of the six coffins.

The room was still empty.

Winchflat sank to the ground, buried his face in his hands and began to cry.

'Nobody loves me,' he wailed. 'Not even someone I manufactured.'

'She can't have gone far,' said Betty, patting her weeping brother on the shoulder.

'But I gave her everything,' Winchflat sobbed. 'My very best titanium nut and bolt through her neck. I thought, should I use an ordinary steel nut and bolt seeing as how this is my first attempt? But no, I used the best of everything, spared no expense, no tacky version of Windows to program her brain. I used the best Apple operating system. No feeble Bluetooth connection to join all the synapses, I used super Air Port Express and all eighty-seven volumes of the *World Encyclopedia*, including the full-colour maps.'

'Maybe that's the problem,' Betty suggested. 'Maybe all that information and especially the full-colour maps made her run away to see the world.'

'Do you think so?' said Winchflat.

'Could be. Maybe you should have only put a

local street map inside her head. At least until she was house-trained.'

'I have an idea,' said Ffiona.

'Really?' said Betty, Mordonna and Nerlin at once.

'Well, maybe it's not such a good idea,' said Ffiona.

'No, go on,' said Mordonna.

'Well, Betty said that Winchflat was a genius and could build anything . . .' Ffiona started.

'Yes, I did. It's true,' said Betty.

'Well, couldn't you build a tracking machine that could show you where Igorina's gone?' said Ffiona.

'Brilliant,' said Mordonna, Betty and Nerlin.

'Probably,' said Winchflat. 'Though I have a terrible feeling I already know where she is.'

'Oh yes?' said Mordonna. 'Is there something you're not telling us?'

'Umm, well, it's the feet,' said Winchflat.

'The feet?'

'Yes, I used Grandmother's,' said Winchflat. 'I

asked her first. I didn't just take them, and she said it was all right because being buried in the coffin in the back garden she didn't need them.'

'So you think Mummy's feet may have led your creation astray?' said Mordonna.

'Not so much astray,' said Winchflat, 'as home.'

'You mean?'

'Yes, back to Transylvania Waters.'

This, of course, had all sort of terrible implications.

Firstly, it meant that none of them could go and fetch Igorina because Mordonna's father, King Quatorze, had spies everywhere whose entire existence was devoted to finding out where Mordonna was and bringing her back to Transylvania Waters.

Secondly, it meant that if Igorina fell into the wrong hands –the only sort of hands there were in Transylvania Waters – they might be able to use her to lead them back to Acacia Avenue.

'Could you build two machines?' Ffiona

asked. 'One to track her down and another one to program her brain remotely so she thinks she comes from somewhere completely different?'

'Yes, like Belgium,' said Betty.

'It's possible,' said Winchflat. 'Though I'd have to build a third machine to block any machines someone else might make to deprogram my reprogramming.'

'Well, you better get started then, hadn't you,' snapped Mordonna.

'And to be on the safe side I'd better build an anti-deprogramming-reprogramming-monitor with a cloaking device just to make sure everything goes to plan.'

'How long is all that going to take?' said Mordonna. 'I have a terrible feeling we're going to have to move a long, long way away.'

'At least until dinner time,' said Winchflat.

'What,' said Betty, 'you mean you could build all four machines in three hours?'

'Of course I'll have to leave the safety warnings off and use cardboard instead of welded steel, but

I should be able to do it OK,' said Winchflat. 'Though it would help if we had dinner a little bit later tonight.'

'How much later?' asked Mordonna, who liked to get dinner on, near or under the table on the dot of seven.

'About three weeks.'

'WHAT?!'

'Just joking,' said Winchflat and then, looking a bit confused, added, 'At least, I think I was.'

'What do you mean you think you were?' said Mordonna.

'Well, I've never made one before,' said Winchflat.

'What, one of those machines?'

'No, a joke.'

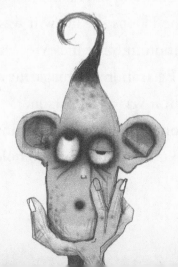

'I wish Betty worked at your father's office,' said Mrs Hulbert the next morning when her husband had gone off to work.

She was about to start ironing Ffiona's socks – which she always did since her own mother had done it for her and old habits die hard – but since meeting the Floods she knew it was time to invite Mr Relaxation into her life. Mrs Hulbert had read about Mr Relaxation in a magazine and for months she thought it was a real person.

Not only would she stop ironing socks, but she would also use a rubber band to hold her hair back

instead of twenty-four hair pins. In fact, she might even think about the possibility of considering the idea of spending a whole day without holding her hair back at all, though of course she would have to make sure that no one except her family saw her.

'Why?' said Ffiona.

'I'm not supposed to tell you this, but your father is having a terrible time. You know how you used to get treated at Thistlecrown? Well, that's how they treat your father at work,' said Mrs Hulbert.

'What, you mean they flush him down the toilet?'

'No. I think they tried once, but he wouldn't fit,' said Mrs Hulbert. 'But how his boss acts is just as bad.'

Ffiona felt really sad. Her dad was a kind, quiet man who wouldn't hurt a fly. In fact, he caught flies and, instead of squashing them like most people would, or eating them like the Floods did, he took them out into the garden and gave them their freedom. Of course, most of the time freedom meant the opportunity to fly straight back inside the Hulberts' house and carry on eating the chocolate icing on Mrs Hulbert's cake, which they'd been doing when Mr Hulbert had grabbed them in the first place. Then Mr Hulbert would sigh and take the fly outside all over again. This could happen five or six times before Mrs Hulbert would squash the fly when her husband wasn't looking.

That's how kind Mr Hulbert was – and he never complained, either. It had taken him several years to tell his wife he was having a bad time at work.

'So you have to promise me that you won't let him know I told you, all right?' said Mrs Hulbert.

'All right, Mum. But maybe Betty *could* help him,' said Ffiona.

'No, sweetheart. It's not like school,' said Mrs Hulbert, regretting she'd said anything. 'Your father could lose his job.'

'But . . .'

'No, promise me that none of this is to leave the room,' Ffiona's mother insisted.

In that case I'll have to get Betty to come here. Then I can tell her in this room, Ffiona said to herself, though she had already decided to tell her friend anyway, because if anyone would know what to do it would be Betty.

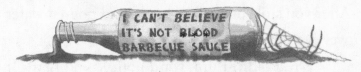

'First of all,' Betty said when Ffiona told her, 'we have to find out exactly what the problem is.'

'Yes, but how do we do that? We can't just go to my dad's office and see what's happening.'

'No, we can't,' said Betty, 'but Winchflat will help us. He'll invent something.'

They went back to Betty's house, but as usual Winchflat was nowhere to be found. This was why Mordonna had made her son install a special Winchflat-Summoning-Button in the kitchen. If she hadn't he would have missed every single meal and probably starved to death because he was not the sort of boy who snacked between meals, apart from the odd beetle or earwig.

'Is it dinner time already?' said Winchflat as he arrived in the kitchen.

'No,' said Betty. 'It was me. We need your help.'

'Why should I help you?' Winchflat asked. 'After you stole one of my books and poured water over everything.'

'Oh, I didn't think you'd notice,' said Betty. 'I was just trying to help my friend. Sorry.'

Betty's magic may have left a lot to be desired, but when she tilted her head down a bit, fluttered her eyelids and said 'sorry' in a really small pathetic

voice, almost everyone – except her mother, who had taught her the trick – fell under her spell.

'OK, little sister, just for you,' said Winchflat. He went straight to his secret cellar.

He locked himself in and sat in his magic chair.

DANGER!!

This chair eats little babies and puppies.

Counting backwards from twenty-seven, he pressed a combination of buttons on a key pad and vanished. He reappeared in his secret, secret cellar that no one knew about. It was hidden in the last place anyone would ever look for a cellar – up in the roof – and it was here that Winchflat kept his most secret experiments and his bizarre collection of very weird creatures.

'Angela, I have a job for you,' he said to a ball-point pen.

'Yes, master,' said Angela, who obviously was not a ball-point pen or she wouldn't have been able to speak.

Winchflat explained that he would give Angela to Ffiona, who would give Angela to her father to take to work, where she was to record everything that went on that day.

'If there's a problem, simply send me a distress signal,' said Winchflat and, pointing to a red button on his shirt, he added, 'One press of this emergency button and you will be beamed back here in an instant.'

'No problem, oh great creator,' said Angela. 'It will be good to get out and do some real work instead of sitting round here trying to make intelligent conversation with the pencils. If I have to listen to that wretched 2B or not 2B joke again, I'll burst my ink tanks.'

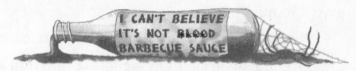

'Right then,' Winchflat said as he re-appeared in the kitchen. 'This is Angela and she will send us a report of what's happening in your father's office. 'Don't tell your dad. Just let him think Angela's an ordinary pen.'

'OK,' said Ffiona and, looking at Angela, she added, 'You can write like an ordinary pen, can't you?'

'Duhhh,' said Angela, 'yeah, in black and red, and I can do self-correcting spelling in fifteen languages. I can't do Belgian, of course. I'm not that sort of pen.'

Ffiona gave Angela to her dad that evening.

This confused him because it wasn't Christmas or his birthday, which were the two days he was usually given pens.

'You didn't do anything wrong, like steal it, did you?' said Mr Hulbert.

'No, of course not,' said Ffiona. 'I, um, Betty gave it to me.'

'It's not a magic pen, is it?' said Mr Hulbert. 'It's not going to do anything weird like turn into a werewolf or start talking to me?'

Angela bit her refill, which is like biting your tongue if you're human. It was all she could do not to speak.

'Dad, it's a pen,' said Ffiona. 'I thought you might like to use it at work.'

'Oh no,' said Mr Hulbert. 'I don't think I'd better take it to work. It's much too smart. Someone might take it.'

Angela sent an emergency signal to Winchflat, who made a few instant adjustments. Angela's gold clip turned chrome and her shiny blue lacquer changed into a dull grey with a few scratches.

It's only for now, Winchflat said inside Angela's brain. *When this is over I'll make you gorgeous again.*

'It's just an ordinary pen, Dad,' said Ffiona.

'So it is,' said her dad and put it in his jacket pocket between two cheap plastic biros, who kept Angela awake all night talking about ink.

'Got your new pen, Dad?' said Ffiona the next morning as Mr Hulbert was leaving for work.

'Yes, sweetheart, but I'm still not sure I should take it with me,' Mr Hulbert replied.

'It'll bring you good luck,' said Ffiona.

'OK, sweetheart, just to make you happy.'

When he reached his office, Mr Hulbert laid Angela on his desk. Within five minutes Mr Gross, Mr Hulbert's bullying boss, stopped in front of him, picked Angela up and stirred his tea with her.

'Oh dear, Halibut,[33] I hope I haven't hurt your new pen,' he said.

Angela screamed. Her voice was too high for

---

[33] *A halibut is a type of fish. Mr Gross, who lived up to his name, always called Mr Hulbert halibut.*

humans to hear, but Winchflat detected it on his equipment and sent her a special spell for cooling down boiled ball-points. Because he was always prepared for every single eventuality, Winchflat had actually created the spell a few days earlier, along with a cleaning spell to remove earwax from the end of pens when people stuck them in their ears to clean them out. This was exactly what Gross did next.

'Good pen, that,' he said. He waited for Mr Hulbert to say he could have it, but Mr Hulbert didn't.

'My d-d-daughter gave it to m-m-me,' he said.

'Your daughter!' sneered Gross. 'I didn't know you had a license to breed, Halibut.'

Mr Hulbert, as usual, said nothing. He bent his head over his paperwork and waited for Gross to go away.

'Fancy that, everyone,' said Gross. 'The halibut's been breeding.'

The office looked embarrassed, but no one said a word.

'I always thought you lived under a stone,' Gross continued. 'I find it hard to believe there's a Mrs Hulbert.'

He went on like that for another five minutes before walking off, taking Angela with him. While all this had been going on, Angela had been transmitting every detail back to Winchflat. Gross went in to his office and sat down at his desk,

putting his feet up on the box he kept under the desk to rest his short legs on.

That was the basis of Mr Gross's problem. He was very short and it made him feel he had to be the boss of everyone. He didn't just need to feel better than everyone else, he needed to try and make them feel much worse than him. Most people who worked for Gross didn't stay longer than a few weeks.

Mrs Hulbert kept telling her husband to leave, but he was too nervous.

'I'm sure things will get better,' he kept saying as his hair began to turn grey and fall out.

But it didn't get better, because angry little men like Gross never let up. Of course, if Mr Hulbert had stood up to him, Gross would have backed down straight away. Cowards always do. But Mr Hulbert was scared he would lose his job so he just put up with all the daily misery.

Angela sat on Gross's desk and watched him. When he picked her up to sign a letter, she dribbled ink all over his shirt front.

174

'It was the least I could do,' she said later.

Gross stormed out of his office, threw Angela at Mr Hulbert and told him he had to buy him a new shirt.

And then something very strange happened.

As Mr Hulbert opened his mouth to apologise, Winchflat transmitted a magic field through Angela.

The words Mr Hulbert's brain created were, 'I'm terribly sorry, sir, what size shirt collar are you?'

The words that came out were, 'I've just about had enough of you, you evil little poisoned toad.'

The whole office fell so silent that you could hear a pin drop. Gross stood rooted to the spot with his mouth opening and closing and nothing coming out.

Mr Hulbert tried to apologise. Instead of saying how sorry he was and how he didn't know what had come over him and straight after work he would go and buy not one, but two shirts, what he actually said was, 'You are the worst boss in the world and it's about time you were taught a lesson.'

The whole office, all twenty-five people, were now standing with their mouths hanging open. Gross was still doing his goldfish impersonation when Angela leapt off Mr Hulbert's desk and squirted ink all over his face and down his trousers – not just ordinary ball-point ink, but very smelly ink that seemed to have been made from dead fish.

Gross tried to scream, except part of Winchflat's magic had been to strike him dumb. He turned to walk back to his office but Angela had also sprayed a pool of ink just behind him, which he slipped in, landing face first in front of the newest secretary, who had already told him she was leaving at the end of the week.

'Here,' she said, 'let me help you get that nasty ink off your face.' And she poured a cup of tea over him.

Up in Winchflat's attic cellar, Betty and Ffiona sat watching on a TV screen that was beaming back everything Angela could see.

'Now what?' said Ffiona. 'Won't my dad get in the most awful trouble?'

'Don't worry about that,' said Winchflat. 'We will now implement the second part of the plan. Come on, get into my shrink-you-as-small-as-a-speck-of-dust-transport-you-somewhere-then-enlarge-you-again-machine.'

'Your what?' said Betty.

'My SYASAASODTYSTEYA machine,' said

Winchflat, reading the letters off a label stuck to his wardrobe door. 'If you can't remember that, just call it the Zoomy Thing.'

'Is that it?' said Betty.

'Yes, brilliant, isn't it?'

'It looks like a wardrobe,' said Ffiona.

'Exactly,' said Winchflat. 'It's even got clothes hanging inside it. That way no one can tell what it really is.'

'You mean it's kind of like the Tardis on *Doctor Who*?' said Betty.

'Apart from the fact that it's a wardrobe and not a phone box and that it is not any bigger inside than it is outside and it doesn't have a blue light on top and it doesn't make funny weird noises when it materialises, I suppose it's exactly like the Tardis,' said Winchflat.

'It's not very original, is it?' said Betty.

'What do you mean?' asked Winchflat.

'A wardrobe. It's just like *The Lion, the Witch and the Wardrobe*, isn't it?'

'No it's not,' said Winchflat. 'There's no lion.'

'Well, why couldn't you use something different, like a chest of drawers?'

'Listen, it's squashed enough inside the wardrobe, what with all the clothes in there,' said Winchflat. 'Can you imagine trying to get inside a

chest of drawers? Anyway, I had a wardrobe. I don't
have a chest of drawers. Now come on, we've got to
hurry and help Ffiona's father.'

'But a wardrobe . . .' said Betty.

'Listen, little sister, this is no ordinary
wardrobe.'

'No more I am,' said the wardrobe. 'I have
held the robes of kings and queens.'

'Come on, get in,' said Winchflat. 'There's no
time to lose.'

'Is it safe?' said Betty.

'Absolutely,' said Winchflat. 'It's as safe as
hearses.'

'Should that be as safe as houses?' said
Ffiona.

'Hopefully, yes,' said Winchflat.

So that all three of them could fit inside the
wardrobe, they had to take out six overcoats and
seventeen pairs of shoes. The wardrobe was not
happy about it and threatened to lock her doors
when Winchflat tried to take out the three hat
boxes.

'Right,' said Winchflat, 'hold on. I'm homing in on Angela's signal and then I'll transport us there.'

'Do we have to hold our breath or shut our eyes?' said Ffiona.

'No, because we'll be there quicker than a split . . .' Winchflat began to say as he pressed the red button.

There was a flash and a smell of burnt onions, which Winchflat apologised for and said he was trying to fix, and the wardrobe vanished. A fraction of a second later it re-materialised in Mr Hulbert's office.

'Right,' said Betty as the three of them climbed out. 'Where's that dreadful man?'

In order to avoid complications later with people saying a wardrobe had appeared out of nowhere, Winchflat's machine transmitted a magic beam that made everyone around it fall sleep. Winchflat clicked his fingers and Mr Hulbert woke up.

'Umm, err, umm,' he said, pointing at the wardrobe. 'Wardrobe, wardrobe, wardrobe, wardrobe.'

'Yes, it is isn't it,' said Winchflat and clicked his fingers again to make Mr Hulbert relax.

Mr Hulbert didn't relax much, but at least he stopped saying wardrobe over and over again. He expected Gross to appear from behind the wardrobe and scream at him, but Gross wasn't so

much standing behind the wardrobe as lying down being very flat and dead underneath it.

Ffiona sat her father down and gave him a glass of water.

'Brilliant,' said Betty.

'But he's dead,' said Ffiona. 'Isn't that wrong and kind of against the law?'

'Normally, yes,' said Winchflat. 'But Gross has simply been transported into another creature. He's not so much dead as now living inside a small green frog deep in the Amazon rainforest. I tried to move him into something cuddly like a rabbit, but because he was so vile he ended up as one of those frogs the Amazon Indians get poison from for their arrows.'

'You just made all that up,' said Betty.

'No I didn't,' said Winchflat. 'It's one of the basic laws of robotics that robots are not allowed to hurt humans, and my Zoomy Thing is a kind of robot and so it transmogrified Mr Gross into something else. The feet and arms you can see

183

sticking out from underneath ZT are merely an empty shell.'

'Fair enough,' said Betty, who didn't believe a word of it, even though it was actually all true.

'Now what I suggest you do,' Winchflat said to Mr Hulbert, 'is phone your head office and tell them that your boss has walked out. It wouldn't

surprise me if, because you've been here much longer than everyone else, they put you in charge.'

'Oh no, I don't think they'd do that,' said Mr Hulbert.

'Yes they will,' said Winchflat. 'Wait until we've gone, count to fifty and then make the phone call.'

Winchflat slipped an exhausted Angela into his pocket, ushered the two girls back into the wardrobe, pressed the green button and they vanished.

'What about the body?' said Betty.

'It's stuck underneath ZT,' said Winchflat. 'We'll give it to Granny when we get home. She'll dispose of it for us.'[34]

'. . . forty-nine, fifty,' said Mr Hulbert and everyone in the office woke up with all memory of the leaking pen incident erased from their memories.

---

[34] *Queen Scratchrot will enjoy eating a dead Mr Gross because a diet of cats, mice and encyclopedia salesmen can get a bit boring no matter how much tomato sauce you use.*

'Gross has left the building,' said Mr Hulbert. 'And the good news is, he's not coming back.'

He rang head office and it was exactly as Winchflat had predicted. Because he had been there so much longer than anyone else, he was put in charge. His wages were doubled. The newest secretary, who had poured the tea over Gross, changed her mind and decided not to leave at the end of the week, and the office started to make five times as much money as it ever had before, which meant everyone got a huge bonus and Mr Hulbert got a company car, which was a bit embarrassing for a while until he learnt how to drive.

'It just goes to show,' said Mrs Hulbert to Ffiona. 'All that nastiness your father put up with over the years has finally been rewarded.'

'Yes, Mother.'

'And you didn't have to ask Betty to help either, did you?'

'No, Mother.'

That weekend, Mr Hulbert put all his cardigans in a pile in the back garden and set fire to

them. The following weekend the whole Hulbert family went to the mall and bought jeans, though Mrs Hulbert drew the line when her husband said he was thinking of getting a tattoo.

Winchflat made a new cellar under number 11 and set up his tracking, cloaking, disguising and confusing machines. The screens were all blank, but as he twiddled the knobs and calibrated the calibratey bits and pressed the hyper-active button, signals began to come through.

At first the screens were filled with rubbish: Vatican TV's edition of *Big Brother*, which is actually called *Little Sister*, a strange sports channel from Outer Mongolia that appeared to involve a lot of men in felt boots jumping up and down in puddles of yak's sick, and a shopping channel

that was so believable that Winchflat found himself phoning up and ordering a body-building machine, which he thought would actually build a body for him and save all the complicated stuff he'd had to do to make Igorina if he ever needed to make another one.

Betty, who had gone down to the cellar to lend a hand, bought herself two sets of genuine imitation diamondette necklaces set in pure 28-carat gold alloy – one set for herself and one for Mordonna.

Finally things settled down and a small red dot appeared on the left of the screen. The dot moved slowly forward and then came to a dead stop not quite in the centre of the screen. Winchflat and Betty held their breaths,[35] waiting for it to move those last few millimetres, but it didn't.

'You're sure that's her, are you?' said Betty.

---

[35] *Wizards can actually take out their breaths and hold them in their hands. They often do it for a laugh at parties to make everyone think they are dead.*

'Oh yes,' said Winchflat. 'I'd recognise her anywhere.'

'But it's just a red dot.'

'Well, it might be just a red dot to you,' Winchflat snapped, 'but it's my Igorina to me.'

'OK, so where is she?'

'Ah, well, now, yes, umm. Where's my calculator?' said Winchflat.

He pressed the calculator to his lips and then held it against the red dot on the screen.

'Aren't you supposed to do sums or something?' said Betty.

'Who's the genius,' said Winchflat, 'you or me?'

'Huh,' Betty snorted. 'You've changed, haven't you? Build yourself a girlfriend and suddenly you've got an attitude. Well, listen, brother, girlfriend or not, you're still a nerdy weirdo.'

Before Winchflat could answer, a special blue light bulb on top of one of the machines started flashing.

'Get down,' said Winchflat. 'Laser coming.'

A loud humming filled the air and a fifty-million watt laser beam lit up the room. It bounced backwards and forwards from wall to wall, wrapped itself round the door handle and came to rest on Winchflat's Zoomy Thing wardrobe, which he had brought along in case they needed to rush round the world after Igorina.

'That's odd,' said Winchflat as he and Betty crouched under a table. 'It's supposed to point a thin beam onto that map on the wall over there and show us where she is.'

The loud humming faded and was replaced by another noise. The noise was like a very, very old hippopotamus with a really bad sore throat trying to laugh at another hippopotamus that has just fallen face down in the mud.[36] Winchflat ran across the room and threw open the wardrobe door.

There was Igorina, doing her best to laugh.

'What are you doing in there, you naughty girl?' said Winchflat.

---

[36] *Which, of course, is something all hippos do at least three times a day.*

'Sideunheek,' said Igorina, who still needed a lot of lessons in speech therapy, starting with Lesson One: Open Your Mouth.[37]

Winchflat reached into the wardrobe, grabbed hold of Igorina's hands, and helped her out. This was not a good idea because one of her hands came off in his hand, making Igorina laugh so much that indescribable purple stuff started coming out of her nose. Betty, who was much better at sewing than her brother, stitched the hand back on and then went over Igorina, adding extra stitches here and there to make sure everything stayed in the right place. The purple stuff crawled off and hid in the corner, where it began to mutate.[38]

---

[37] *My grandson Walter, who is eight months old, has just learned to say Mama and Dada, but he is still learning to remember to open his mouth* before *he says the word and not halfway through.*

[38] *A small ant that was also in the corner looked at the mutating purple stuff and thought,* It'll end in tears. *Which it may well do in another book because that's the sort of thing that happens with purple stuff.*

'I recognise this ear,' said Betty as she fixed it on more securely with a few staples.

'Yes, it's one of mine,' said Winchflat. 'I read in a magazine that nothing says "I love you" like giving someone one of your ears.'

'That is gross,' said Betty.

'Don't knock it until you've tried it,' said Winchflat. 'Just you wait until you get older and get a boyfriend. You might want to give him one of your ears.'

'Well, it didn't work for Van Gogh,' said Betty.

'Who?'

'Never mind.'

'Anyway, little sister, I'm a wizard, remember? I can grow another one.'

Winchflat tightened Igorina's neck bolt and the three of them went to the kitchen at number 13, where Mordonna was cooking dinner. Being a very caring mother, she had actually downloaded some special recipes from the internet on things to cook for newly created Frankenstein type monsters.

When she tasted the Rusty-Girder and Festering-Foot Risotto Igorina's face broke out in a big grin, but Winchflat managed to fix it back together with some gaffer tape.

'That was a close shave,' said Mordonna. 'You'll have to be more careful in future, Winchflat. And I think you'd better give Grandma her feet back, just in case your creation does decide to go walkabout again.'

'What will I use for Igorina?' said Winchflat. 'I mean, I can't expect her to sit down all day.'

'Well, you're the inventor. You'll think of something.'

As luck would have it, *Frankenstein* was just one of a

whole box of old black and white films Winchflat had been given. One of the others was *The Wizard of Oz*, which he also thought was a documentary. The Tin Man gave him an idea.

Using seven old baked bean tins and some pop rivets, he made Igorina a pair of metal feet.

At first she kept tripping over – not because she couldn't walk in them properly, but because Winchflat had forgotten to wash out the cans and small animals kept trying to eat the baked bean juice

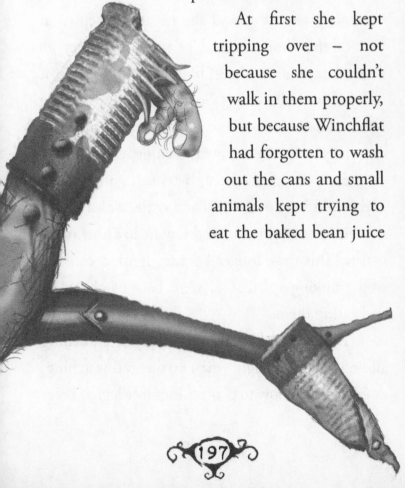

that was oozing out between Igorina's toes. She also drove everyone crazy with the terrible noise she made walking everywhere, until Winchflat glued some bits of car tyre under her feet.

Gradually, as all the stitches took hold and the various bits joined together in a more or less permanent way, Igorina worked her way into everyone's affections and she became accepted as part of the family instead of something they all wanted to put in the rubbish bin. However, it did take a while to get Satanella to stop pulling Igorina's hands off and burying them in the garden, especially as Igorina seemed to enjoy it.

Each day after school, Betty sat Igorina down and taught her how to read and write. At least once a week Ffiona joined in and taught her how to do maths. This took longer because Igorina couldn't stop thinking calculators were bars of chocolate and eating them.

The twins, who secretly enjoyed gardening and only did it at night when no one was watching, taught Igorina how to plant things by digging holes

with a shovel, and not with her teeth held in her left hand, as Igorina tried to do at first.

Merlinmary just made her giggle by giving her friendly electric shocks of a few million volts, while Valla introduced her to the joys of blood.

Of course, Winchflat was over the moon at having a mad assistant to help him with his experiments, just like Doctor Frankenstein had in the movie. Whatever Igorina did, Winchflat simply adored her all the more, even when she was helping him build complex and delicate machines and she muddled things up, like pouring a litre of boiling oil into a very complicated and fragile computer instead of handing him the small screwdriver he'd asked her for.

Mordonna, wisely, decided not to teach Igorina how to cook. She tried to teach her how to wash up but no one would eat anything off the plates after she had washed them, because, being a waterwise creature, Igorina cleaned everything by putting it into her mouth and sucking all the old food off. She even got Winchflat to modify the end

of her tongue so she could get the hard-to-reach bits stuck between the prongs of the forks.

Nerlin decided that the only thing he could teach Igorina to do was to wash and polish the car, which didn't take long because the Floods didn't have a car. Mr Hulbert had a company car, now, though, so Igorina went round to their house every Friday night and cleaned it. This also involved re-spraying the car because she was so enthusiastic at cleaning the dirt off that she cleaned all the paint off too. All the neighbours thought the Hulberts had become rather eccentric because they seemed to have a different coloured car *every* week.

Mrs Hulbert had to have a long lie down after she showed Igorina how to do embroidery and the creature had sewn all her fingers together.

'Though I must say,' Mrs Hulbert admitted, 'she did it with very neat stitches and in exquisite colours.'

'I suppose it comes from having been sewn together herself,' said Mordonna.

The two families were sitting on the Floods'

back verandah drinking slurpies, some of which did not contain body parts. It was a warm summer's Friday night and everyone was feeling very relaxed.

'You know what would be nice?' said Mordonna.

'What's that, my darling?' said Nerlin.

'A nice holiday at the seaside,' said Queen Scratchrot from inside her coffin.[39]

'Once again, Mother, you have read my thoughts,' said Mordonna.

'We could all go,' said Nerlin. 'Both families.'

'What a great idea,' said Mr and Mrs Hulbert.

---

[39] *The queen has a small mouthpiece that she attaches to the end of her rat-soup funnel so people who can't hear her inside their heads can also hear what she is saying.*

Epilogue

Even though Betty and Ffiona had borrowed the *How To Teach Magic To Someone Who May Or May Not Have A Bit Of Wizard's Blood In Their Veins* book from Winchflat, it was agreed by everyone that Ffiona was quite magical enough already and there was no need to perform any spells on her. This was great relief to everyone, especially Ffiona, who had realised quite a while ago that what happened when Betty did magic was only very remotely connected to what she had meant to happen.

Betty had to spend three days in Winchflat's library ironing all the wet books until they were dry.

Then she had to spend another three days mending all the books she had set on fire when she had tried to use a very small dragon with the flame turned down really low, but not as low as she had thought, to help her do the drying.

And in case you were wondering what life was like at Sunnyview School after Bridie had been thrown out and all the other bullies had quietly changed their ways, it was like a lot of school: too boring to write about.

Spot The Difference

BEFORE

SAD

TOTALLY NOT

Mum & Dad
looking about
20 years older
than they
really are.

DUMMY

DULL AND GREY

Nearly Invisible

I had a big problem drawing this page. Because the Hulberts
used to be SO boring I kept falling asleep while I was drawing
the 'Before' bit. So I couldn't show you ALL the 2,873
differences. It doesn't really matter because 2,837 of them are
the extra hairs in Mr Hulbert's trendy new beard.

AFTER

TOTALLY COOL

Mum & Dad looking, like, totally at least, yeah, like 10 years younger than they, like, are. Yeah. LOL.

TAPE MEASURES RULE

iPod

Happy

Bright and Sunny

One of the differences you might not have noticed is that now the Hulberts are actually a bit bigger.

WHAT HAIR

INCORPORATING
HAIRY WOMAN'S WEEKLY

"BAN BALDIES"
SAYS
HAIRY SPICE

OUR TOP TEN

HAIR RECIPES

In This Month's Issue
- Hair of the dog soup.
- Knit your own rat hair tongue-warmer.
- Hairy eggs: will they catch on?
- Can swallowing a hair strangle your heart? A doctor replies.
- Dandruff collecting for fun and profit.
- Part 83 of our popular 'Hairs of the Rich and Famous'.

EAL or FAKE?

Professor Erasmus Follicle of The Hobart Hair Institute claims this is a photo of three hairballs found inside a sample of rock collected on Mars and is proof of life in outer space. Our own Dr Gland says it is a fake and probably no more than a magnified photo of a family of Patagonian Earwigs worn by ancient witches to keep their ears warm during the long winter nights. You be the judge!

Now turn to the next page for our fascinating article on Hair Juggling!!

Did YOU miss these?
THE FLOODS 1, 2 & 3

THE FLOODS

1

NEIGHBOURS

Everybody needs good neighbours . . .

The Floods aren't like other families – for a start, they're all witches and wizards. And they weren't made in the traditional way like you or me. Some of Nerlin and Mordonna Flood's six eldest children were made in the cellar, using an ancient recipe book and a very big turbocharged wand. The youngest child, Betty, is a normal, pretty little girl – but her attempts at magic never go the way she plans.

The next-door neighbours should have known better than to annoy a family of witches and wizards. But they did, and they're about to find out what the Floods do to bad neighbours.

THE FLOODS
2
PLAYSCHOOL

Look through a murky arched window in deepest Patagonia, and this is what you might see . . .

Every day five of the Flood children travel halfway round the world to Quicklime College, the ultimate school for witches and wizards. There's no time for silly games flying around on broomsticks. Sports day is coming up, and before you even wonder how four-legged Satanella copes with the three-legged race, here's a secret for you. Orkward Warlock, the vilest child in the school, and his sidekick, The Toad, hate the big happy Floods family. And they're plotting to kill the Floods – on sports day.

THE FLOODS
3
HOME & AWAY

The Floods family are on the run!

Travel back in time to faraway Transylvania Waters and find out what happened when a lowly drain cleaner called Nerlin Flood fell in love with the royal princess Mordonna. Can the two escape from an explosively angry King Quatorze, the nastiest spies in the land, and the prospect of life down the toilet? Why does their eldest child, Valla, drink blood? Was Satanella really turned into a dog because of an accident with a prawn and a faulty wand? This is your chance to find out how all the Floods children came to be born – or created.

How Much Blood and Fear Can YOU Handle?

THE FLOODS
5

PRIME
SUSPECT

It was a dark and moonless night and in the darkness something stirred . . .

OUT NOW!

The body had obviously been dead for a while. Grass had started growing out of its nose and a family of Patagonian Pocket Mice had built a nest in one of the jacket sleeves.

CSI special investigator Septic took out his blue torch and shone it in the corpse's face. The body was out in broad daylight so the torch light was barely visible, but the blue torch was always the first thing Septic used at a crime scene and rules were rules, especially in forensic science.

Putting on a pair of rubber gloves, Septic began to go through the victim's pockets.

'Interesting,' he said, holding up a small brown object and handing it to his assistant, Oily. 'Bag this.'

Oily put the object in his mouth and sucked it. He rolled it around with his tongue, frowned, sucked it some more then swallowed it.

'I said bag it, not eat it,' said Septic. 'I wanted it analysed back in the lab.'

'No need, boss,' said Oily. 'I can tell you all you need to know. Treacle toffee from a small town in Belgium. Unlike normal Belgian treacle toffee, which is made with one hundred percent local products, this one has been tampered with. It contained treacle from Transylvania Waters.'

'How can you be so sure?' Septic asked.

'Because only Transylvania Waters treacle contains lethal amounts of arsenic,' said Oily and dropped down dead.

'Fair enough,' said Septic.

This sort of thing happened all the time and the Crime Scene Investigation department always kept at least ten Oily clones on hand to cover the sudden assistant-becoming-dead situations that occurred about four times a week. Septic spoke into his phone and a couple of minutes later an identical assistant arrived.

'Your first observation?' said Septic.

'Our killer was a very considerate person,' said Oily.

'How so?'

'Well, look where we are, chief,' Oily replied. 'In the school graveyard. I mean, we've got less than ten metres to go to bury the body.'

'That's another thing,' said Septic. 'Don't you think it's strange for a school to have a graveyard?'

The two investigators and the dead body were standing at the entrance to the graveyard at Quicklime College, the famous yet very secretive school where all the students were witches and wizards apart from a few ghosts and ogres.[1] This was the school where five of the Flood children went every day.

And the dead body *was* standing, not lying down like dead people are supposed to. It was leaning against the left stone gatepost with an absent-minded expression on its face as if it had been waiting for a bus rather than being in a becoming-dead situation. What made the

---

[1] *There were not enough ghosts and ogres of school age to support a school of their own so they were allowed to study at Quicklime's along with the regular students and the Smith-Klaxon cannibal triplets.*

scene even more mysterious was that the victim, although dead in Patagonia in South America, had half a return ticket clutched in his left hand for the journey from Bruges Town Hall to the city morgue, which was many thousands of kilometres away in Europe.[2]

'So, do you think the victim was Belgian, chief?' said Oily.

'Possibly,' said Septic. 'Though of course, he could have been a bus ticket collector.'

This turned out to be the case, because a search of all the victim's pockets turned up bus tickets from eighteen other countries, including Wales and Tristan da Cunha, which doesn't even have a bus service . . .

---

[2] *Of course, bright readers will know already that Patagonia is in South America and that Bruges is a town in Belgium, which in Europe, and that the two countries are on opposite sides of the world, but unfortunately some of you might have teachers who know a bit less about geography than a blind upside-down cave fish and who think Bruges are those purple marks you get on your skin when you bang yourself.*

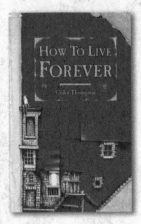

If you liked this book, there's heaps more stuff to check out at

www.thefloods.com.au

- ▶ Games
- ▶ Quizzes
- ▶ Downloads
- ▶ Character profiles

Books are just the start!

www.randomhouse.com.au

[5]